Sam Looked Dangerous.
Confidence Radiated From Him
In White-Hot Heat.

He said nothing but drew her onto the dance floor, then into his arms.

Dana lifted her face, determined not to let him see how he unnerved her. "So. The prodigal returns at last."

His eyes softened. Warmed. "How are you?"

"I'm well," she said, aware of his thighs brushing hers as they danced. "Where have you been, Sam?"

"You want fifteen years condensed into a paragraph?"

"Why are you here?"

"It's a long story."

His hand slid a little farther across her lower back, bringing her closer. His thumb brushed her spine through the silk of her dress.

"I have time for a long story," she said, her voice catching on the last word.

Dear Reader,

Thanks so much for choosing Silhouette Desire—*the* destination for powerful, passionate and provocative love stories. Things start heating up this month with Katherine Garbera's *Sin City Wedding*, the next installment of our DYNASTIES: THE DANFORTHS series. An affair, a secret child, a quickie Las Vegas wedding…and that's just the beginning of this romantic tale.

Also this month we have the marvelous Dixie Browning with her steamy *Driven to Distraction*. Cathleen Galitz brings us another book in the TEXAS CATTLEMAN'S CLUB: THE STOLEN BABY series with *Pretending with the Playboy*. Susan Crosby's BEHIND CLOSED DOORS miniseries continues with the superhot *Private Indiscretions*. And Bronwyn Jameson takes us to Australia in *A Tempting Engagement*.

Finally, welcome the fabulous Roxanne St. Claire to the Silhouette Desire family. We're positive you'll enjoy *Like a Hurricane* and will be wanting the other McGrath brothers' stories. We'll be bringing them to you in the months to come as well as stories from Beverly Barton, Ann Major and *New York Times* bestselling author Lisa Jackson. So keep coming back for more from Silhouette Desire.

More passion to you!

Melissa Jeglinski

Melissa Jeglinski
Senior Editor
Silhouette Desire

Please address questions and book requests to:
Silhouette Reader Service
U.S.: 3010 Walden Ave., P.O. Box 1325, Buffalo, NY 14269
Canadian: P.O. Box 609, Fort Erie, Ont. L2A 5X3

PRIVATE INDISCRETIONS

SUSAN CROSBY

Published by Silhouette Books
America's Publisher of Contemporary Romance

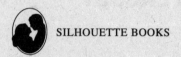 **SILHOUETTE BOOKS**

ISBN 0-373-76570-3

PRIVATE INDISCRETIONS

Copyright © 2004 by Susan Bova Crosby

Visit Silhouette at www.eHarlequin.com

Printed in U.S.A.

SUSAN CROSBY

believes in the value of setting goals, but also in the magic of making wishes. A longtime reader of romance novels, Susan earned a B.A. in English while raising her sons. She lives in the central valley of California, the land of wine grapes, asparagus and almonds. Her checkered past includes jobs as a synchronized swimming instructor, personnel interviewer at a toy factory and trucking company manager, but her current occupation as a writer is her all-time favorite.

Susan enjoys writing about people who take a chance on love, sometimes against all odds. She loves warm, strong heroes; good-hearted, self-reliant heroines…and happy endings.

Readers are welcome to write to her at P.O. Box 1836, Lodi, CA 95241.

For the BABs, Karol, Kathy, Luann and Georgia.
Here's to getting snowed in, good food, great conversation,
Darcy and Bridget—and that's just the beginning.

One

An hour before Sam Remington graduated from high school fifteen years ago, he stuffed the sum of his belongings into three grocery sacks and flung them onto the back seat of his 1977 oil-eating Pacer. Five minutes after the ceremony ended he made his final trip through town, his tailpipe spewing a noxious farewell of good riddance.

Today he returned in a black Mercedes so new it didn't have plates. He'd paid cash for it. But Sam wasn't here to advertise his success to the people he left behind. Normally he wasn't one to dwell on the past. Today was different. He'd chosen the day of his return to his hometown specifically. Certainly he could have come another time. Maybe *should* have. But news of his fifteen-year high-school reunion set the date for him. Some unfinished business of his had gone ignored for too long. He had two people to see. He'd just come from seeing the first one. Now he would deal with the other.

Sam negotiated the winding roads of Miner's Camp, a

community of 3,100 people nestled in the Northern California foothills of the Sierra Nevadas. He kept his gaze straight ahead as he passed the turnoff leading to the house where he was raised—the house from which he'd escaped—although the unusually cool August evening took him back to the nights of his childhood, when he'd roamed the countryside, looking for something he never found.

He ignored the bruising memories and headed to the Elks Lodge. The parking lot was full, the fence posts dotted with red and gold balloons, the colors of Prospector High School, which served a community of several small towns.

Sam pulled off the road and slowed to a stop, gravel crunching under his tires. The party was well under way. Laughter spilled from the open doorways and windows as Madonna sang the 1980s classic "Like a Virgin."

Nostalgia didn't overtake him—he'd never understood the appeal of reunions—still, there was that one person he'd come to see. Only one out of a graduating class of eighty-seven. He was sure she would be in the crowd. And he had something to say to her. To Dana Cleary. Dana Sterling, he amended. Her married name. Then he could close the book on his past forever.

He had a choice in the timing. He could wait until the party ended and catch her at her parents' house, where she would undoubtedly spend the night. Or he could get it over with now and be in San Francisco for his latest assignment before midnight, his past shoveled six feet under....

After a moment Sam turned off the ignition and got out of the car. He'd been in some tight circumstances, life-and-death situations. He'd welcomed the challenges, gloried in the risks, exulted in his escapes. He could channel the adrenaline flow in his body deliberately, but the anticipation of seeing Dana sent a rush through him that he couldn't control. He wondered at the rare sensation, even savored it.

He approached the building but stopped short of entering, waiting for his internal anticipation to settle. Lingering near an open door he noted more balloons, and a disco ball that dappled the room with speeding stars. Memories washed over him of his junior year and another dance. Watching through a window. Music and laughter, dinner and dancing. A longing so painful…

He'd taken her to the senior prom the next year, but their relationship hadn't changed for having gone to the dance.

None of that mattered fifteen years later as Sam slipped into the Elks Lodge just as the deejay took a break from his chatter and the 1980s music. Candi James bounded onto the stage and scooped up the microphone, the same pep-squad perkiness she'd had in high school still evident as she read from a long list, leading the cheers for such notable accomplishments as who had the most children, who'd come the farthest and on and on and on.

With everyone's attention directed at Candi, Sam moved around the perimeter of the room. He stopped when he spotted Dana. He didn't fight the initial jolt of seeing her again, taking a moment to watch her instead. A little taller than average, she was more angular than curvy, her hair not strictly blond or brunette but a honeyed mix of both, and shoulder length now, not the rich waterfall to her waist that had made him want to wrap his hands in it and pull her close.

He couldn't see her eyes from where he stood, but he knew they were obsidian, pitch-dark eyes that had issued him challenges since elementary school.

She wore an unrevealing, blue couture dress and low heels, understated, practical and elegant, befitting her position, but a far cry from the hot-pink number she'd worn at the junior prom.

"And finally," Candi said, folding her list and setting it aside, "our three mega success stories. Harley Bonner, who owns the eighth largest ranching operation in the state of California."

Cheers went up. Sam's blood froze. If he were a vengeful man—

"Lilith Perry Paul, whose radio talk show is now in syndication all over the country.'' More hoots and hollers. ''And finally, Dana Cleary Sterling. Dana—you've made us so proud. Here's to six more years!''

So, Sam thought, the speculation was over. She'd made a decision.

''We'll have music and dancing for two more hours,'' Candi shouted over the din. ''Don't forget the picnic in the park tomorrow at noon. If you haven't had your picture taken for the memory book, you've only got a half hour left. Remember to sign the update forms, too. Have fun!''

Sam watched as well-wishers surrounded Dana, who seemed surprisingly uneasy at the attention. A barrier went up, an invisible wall that kept people at a distance. She held her wineglass in both hands, a silent signal. No handshakes, please. No hugs. Only her friend Lilith got close enough to bump arms, and that lasted but a second.

The change in her surprised him. When had she become so reserved? When had she lost the outward joy of life? She'd touched people. Him.

The music started again, Sting singing ''Every Breath You Take,'' blasting Sam with fresh images of the junior prom where he'd painfully watched Dana with her date, her smile bright. She hadn't been a cheerleader, but almost everything else, including student-body president. She'd seemed golden to him, the way she combined academics, sports and extracurricular activities.

Sam shouldered his way past the memories and through the crowd. Conversation quieted enough for him to hear the reaction being voiced at his appearance.

''Who—''

''I think that's Sam Remington—''

''Really? But he's so—''

''Gorgeous. Can't be Sam. He never dressed that good.''

''He sure has filled out.''

Sam never broke stride. When he did, the murmuring stopped. Surprised pleasure stole across Dana's face, startling him. The anger he'd harbored for years broke loose from its moorings, leaving only what had been good between them.

He put his hand out to her, invading her invisible barrier. Then he waited. The next move was hers.

If it hadn't been for the unmistakable turquoise-colored eyes, Dana wouldn't have recognized him. Gone was the gangly boy. In his place stood a man who commanded attention without saying a word.

She'd looked for him at the five-year and ten-year reunions, more hopeful than she cared to admit. The sharp impact of seeing him now rendered her speechless.

He'd grown, in every way. He looked…dangerous. Confidence radiated from him in white-hot heat. In a room of sport coats and khakis he wore black jeans and a leather jacket. In an evening where no one had gotten too close, he'd come within a foot and put his hand out in such a way that she could either shake it or be led onto the dance floor.

She wanted to dance, but did he? Her dilemma made her heart pound—she'd rejected five other offers. How would it look if she danced with him now? She saw challenge in his eyes. His hand moved fractionally closer to her.

Dana realized she couldn't take any more time to analyze his motives, so she passed her wineglass to Lilith and put her hand in Sam's. She'd waited fifteen years for the chance to talk to him.

"I'd love to dance," she said, maintaining a smile.

He said nothing but drew her onto the dance floor then into his arms, leaving an acceptable amount of space between their bodies. Even so, she hadn't been this intimate with a man in over two years, and then it had been a comfortable closeness, not this…this breath-stealing turmoil.

She lifted her face, determined not to let him see how he unnerved her. She'd gotten so good at controlling her emotions, it had become cold habit, but now his gaze held hers long enough for her lips to tremble. He exuded control—in his eyes, his posture, the firm touch of his hands. She wanted to shake that control, although she had no idea why. She hated it when someone tried to shake hers.

"So," she said, making herself smile. "The prodigal Brainiac returns at last."

His eyes softened. Warmed. "How are you, Blush?"

Their use of their old nicknames brought instant intimacy. She felt herself blushing, then his knowing smile took her back, moments tumbling into other moments.

"I'm well," she said, coming aware of his thighs brushing hers now and then as they danced. "Where have you been, Sam?"

"You want fifteen years condensed into a paragraph?"

"Have you done so little?" she asked lightly, surprising herself. She was flirting and couldn't stop it.

"I've lived."

The way he said the words gave her pause. She would bet the long version of the story would be fascinating. "Start at the beginning, then. Where'd you go after graduation?"

"I joined the army."

Shock left her momentarily at a loss for words. "Why?"

"The opportunity presented itself."

Which made no sense. According to the math teacher, Mr. Giannini, Sam had been destined for greatness in the math community. "Brilliant" had always preceded his name. She shook her head. "Every year when the Nobel Prizes are awarded I look for your name."

"Things change."

"You didn't attend your father's funeral." She remembered how pitiful it had been. So few people, and none who genuinely mourned.

"You did."

So. He'd left, but he'd kept track. "Why are you here, Sam?"

"To thank you."

"For attending the funeral?"

"No."

She looked away, shaken by the intensity of his gaze. Gratitude was the last thing Dana expected. He'd been furious at her at graduation, rightfully so. And she hadn't been allowed to set the record straight or beg forgiveness. By the time she could hunt for him after the ceremony, he'd left town.

"How can you thank me?" The effort to appear casual for the interested bystanders sent her pulse dancing. "Because of me you were beaten. You could barely walk at graduation. Your eye was swollen shut. That was my fault."

"It changed my life, Dana, in ways I never could have anticipated."

How could he be so calm? She wanted to scream, *Mine, too! It changed my life, too.* "Tell me how," she said.

"It's a long story."

His hand slid a little farther across her lower back, bringing her closer. His thumb brushed her spine through the silk of her dress.

"I have time for a long story," she said, her voice catching on the last word as he pressed a finger against a vertebra. When had that spot become an erogenous zone?

"I don't. I've already stayed longer than I intended. Not to mention that everyone in this room is watching our every move."

She pulled back a little. "I guess I'm used to living under a microscope."

"And I'm used to putting people under one."

"Now there's a cryptic comment. Care to explain?"

"No."

The song was ending. Panicked she would miss her opportunity, she hurried her words. She only had seconds to say what she'd been wanting to all these years. "I was sorry, Sam. You protected me and got hurt because of it. I became much more aware of the consequences of my actions after. Much more cautious.''

''Is that why you married Randall Sterling? It was the prudent thing to do?''

Two

Before Dana could come up with a response she stumbled as Sam suddenly stopped dancing. Without releasing her he angled toward the man who'd tapped Sam's shoulder, cutting in. She felt him tense, like an animal facing its prey—or its enemy. Harley Bonner was the enemy. And she'd already turned him down twice tonight.

"Time to share, Remington."

Tightening her grip on Sam, Dana moved closer to him, hoping he would pick up on her unspoken need to avoid Harley—even as she knew it was unfair to expect him to rescue her once again.

"Sharing is an overrated social skill," Sam said as the music switched to "Girls Just Want to Have Fun."

He moved Dana out of range, his hand still resting against the small of her back in a gesture that was both seductive and protective. She didn't know which one appealed to her more.

"Thank you," Dana said, more grateful than she could say. "I'm in your debt. Again."

"We're square. Nobody owes anyone anything." He took his hand away when they reached the edge of the crowd. "I have to go, Dana. It was good seeing you."

Already? She stopped herself from saying the word, grabbing his elbow instead.

"I have your valedictorian medal," she said. "It's at my parents' house." When she'd reached her car after the graduation ceremony she'd found it hanging from her rearview mirror. She'd cried the whole time she spent looking for him. She couldn't believe he'd done that—given her his medal.

"I didn't want it then," he said, "and I don't want it now."

"Please, Sam." She was excruciatingly aware of people dancing and milling around them, although the volume of the music kept their conversation private. And she was so aware of him as a man. "Come with me. It'll just take a few minutes. My parents are out of town. It'd be just you and me."

"I have to go," he repeated.

Was that regret in his eyes? Temptation? Although their unique relationship had begun in elementary school they'd dated only once in high school. Just once. A date she'd dreamed of for years. A date that had started wonderfully and ended abysmally. She never knew what had gone wrong, how she'd ruined the evening, but she had.

She had so many questions to ask him now, had played out the scene in her head so many times. How could he just leave when there were so many unanswered questions?

"I know you don't owe me anything, but at least tell me why you gave me the medal," she said.

"Running away again?" asked a male voice.

Harley ambled up beside them a second time, his chest puffed out, eyes hard, hands fisted. Dana's hatred for him deepened. A bully in high school and a rich bully now.

"Move aside," Sam said, low and threatening.

"Oh ho! Feelin' cocky, are we, Remington? Think you could take me on this time?"

"One on one, I could've beaten you then. Five against one weren't great odds."

Dana hadn't heard the chilling details before. Most people assumed Sam's father had hit him again, but Dana knew Harley and his friends had been responsible. She just didn't know how many people were involved. If she could go back in time, she would handle everything differently.

"Don't make a scene," Dana said to Harley, hurting at the picture of Sam being a punching bag. Because of her. "Just go away."

Harley bristled. "This is my turf. You don't have any power here."

"But I'm wearing my ruby slippers," she said, making an effort to defuse the tension.

He glanced at her feet, not getting the joke. An ominous silence hung between them. Old contentions seemed painfully fresh.

Sam took a step, bringing himself shoulder to shoulder with Harley. "One would think that two ex-wives would've taught you a little something about women and power, Bonner."

Harley drew back his arm. Before Dana could blink, he was on the floor, looking more bewildered than hurt. If Sam threw a punch she hadn't seen it.

"What happened?" someone asked.

"Harley fell, I think," came the response.

Dana felt Sam's gaze on her. She faced him.

"I gather you're running for reelection, six more years. You've got my vote, Senator Sterling," he said, his expression sincere.

"I'll be looking for your contribution."

He smiled at that.

"Are you sure you won't come to the house and get your

medal?'' *Don't go. Please don't go. We have so much to talk about. Regrets. Choices. Dreams.*

He didn't pick up on her unspoken signals this time but dug into his pocket and pulled out a business card. ''You can mail it if that would make you happy.''

''It would.'' She would have his address now. His phone number. Was that worse than not knowing where he was? She remembered something else just as he turned to leave. ''Thank you for the sympathy card you sent after my husband died.''

''I admired him, Dana.'' He held her gaze for a few seconds then strode off.

She could see the military influence in his posture. She knew she couldn't stand there forever watching him go, but she wanted to. Maybe she'd gotten the chance to apologize, as she'd always wanted, but it wasn't finished. He didn't know everything. And now something new intruded—her body's response to him, a kind of sizzling need, down low. A loudly beating heart. A mind spinning with old images and now new ones.

She drew a calming breath as her lifelong friends Lilith, Candi and Willow appeared at her side.

Candi leaned over Harley. ''You know, you should probably have someone take you home so you can sleep it off.'' She angled closer and whispered dramatically, ''I didn't realize your little problem had gotten so out of control.''

Dana was sorry that the conversation had taken the turn it had. She wasn't one to make waves. In fact, she'd dealt with Harley just fine until Sam came along. Sam and the feelings of guilt he brought. Sam and the surprising physical reaction he'd created.

She'd been too long without a man. Without her husband, she amended, having been widowed for more than two years. Two hellish years. Two hectic years. She hadn't had time for dating, given the demands of her job. Nor had anyone interested her enough to make the time. She could make the time for Sam Remington—

"I have a lot of friends," Harley said, his tone vicious. "Friends who will withdraw the financial support you need. Believe me, I won't forget this."

Dana stood her ground as Harley came within inches of her. "Just as I haven't forgotten," she fired back, the memories flooding her, drowning her. What he'd done to her was bad enough. What he'd done to Sam was unforgivable. "I believed your threats before because I was young and naive. Those days are gone."

"You landed on your feet. Bagged yourself a rich, powerful guy. Slipped right into his job like you earned it."

"I was voted in."

"Sympathy. Pity."

Before she could answer, she felt her arm being tugged. Lilith dragged her away. "Look agreeable for your constituents, Senator," Lilith said, moving her across the room, a cool smile on her perfect oval face. "Somebody will gladly pass this incident to the tabloids, you know. A few people have been panting for a moment like this."

"He's blaming me, Lilith. Me. Like he wasn't causing trouble from the beginning tonight." She lowered her voice. "Asking me to dance when he knows I don't want anything to do with him."

"Calm down."

"I'm ready to go."

Lilith patted her arm. "Soon, my dear. You've got to put on a show for a little while longer, then, fortunately for you, you've got me, a seven-months-pregnant friend, to use as an excuse. I'll let Candi and Willow know we'll be leaving a little earlier than we figured."

They'd planned a slumber party like the old days. Dana had been looking forward to it. Now she just wanted to be alone.

It took her an hour to work her way through the curious crowd and another three hours of wine and girl talk before she had time to herself. Dressed in her robe, she wandered out to the front porch and sat in the swing, easing it back and forth, the chain groaning quietly, the motion soothing. Her parents were visiting relatives in Florida, but Dana could feel their presence. How many nights had they sat here, talking and watching the stars?

The peaceful memories tried to wrap her in a quilt of comfort, but her eyes stung at the emotional whirlwind the night had been. The vindictive exchange with Harley and her sexual awareness of Sam put her on edge—she, who was known for her calm, rational behavior. Did he know why she'd apologized or had she been too vague?

Of course, he'd been vague with his thank-you, too.

Dana tucked a hand in her robe pocket to find Sam's business card. She ran her thumb over the gold embossing of the company name, ARC Security & Investigations. She recalled a Los Angeles address, that the card listed phone, fax, cell phone and pager numbers. No title was printed under his name. Because the firm was too small? Maybe even a one-man operation? Sam Remington, Private Investigator. Amazing.

"Can't sleep, either?"

Dana jumped when Lilith settled on the swing.

"I've got a baby break-dancing in my womb. Must be all that 1980s music," Lilith said, a smile in her voice. "What's your excuse?"

"I usually read committee reports as sleep aids. I decided not to bring any paperwork with me this time." Dana nestled her shoulders into the swing cushion and glanced at Lilith. She'd let her hair down, an ebony curtain that trailed down her back. "This is nice," Dana said. "We haven't had any time alone since you got married last year."

"I'm sorry."

"No, don't apologize. It wasn't a criticism. I know what it's like, having a new husband and a demanding career. I missed you, that's all. When you stayed with me for those few weeks after Randall died, I got used to having you around."

They swung in silence for several minutes. Dana closed

her eyes and listened to the night noises of crickets and frogs and other creatures who traveled the forested surroundings. What sounded like a man walking was probably a deer, but it could easily be a fox or raccoon or even a mountain lion.

"Why didn't you tell me you decided to run for reelection?" Lilith asked.

Dana heard the underlying hurt that she wasn't the first of her friends to know. "Candi was wishing out loud. I certainly didn't tell her anything. I haven't even made up my mind." She tried not to cringe at the lie.

"Then, why didn't you correct her?"

"Sam's arrival coincided, I guess. That whole business with Harley." *Lame, Dana. Really lame.* "Would you believe I forgot about it?"

Lilith frowned. "Actually, no. It's totally unlike you."

"I know."

"You're going to be inundated by the media."

"I *know.*"

They slipped into silence again.

"I couldn't believe that Sam showed up," Lilith commented. "He hasn't changed, has he? Drop in unannounced then leave before you know it. Still playing by his own rules. Still keeping his distance."

"What's wrong with having your own rules?"

"Are you defending him?"

Was she? "I liked him. I did go to the prom with him, you know."

"Right. One date. A sympathy date at that."

"Don't say that." When he left without saying goodbye, he'd hurt her in a way like no one had. Still, she had a tender spot for him in her heart. Maybe because she vividly remembered the sad little boy who'd lost his mother when he was ten. Maybe, too, she remembered strong feelings on her part that were never resolved. Her friends hadn't seen that his eyes could sparkle with humor as well as challenge. She'd been a little bit in love with him for years, then the night of the prom had fallen even more—until everything changed, for a reason she never knew.

He was an enigma then, and more so now. Why had he come when he seemed to have no intention of staying beyond a brief conversation with her? And why in such a public forum?

"All I'm saying is that he could've had friends, but he didn't try," Lilith said a little defensively.

"Maybe so. We don't know what he went through with his father, do we? All I know for sure is he did well in school and got out of town when he could. He seems to have made something of himself. He looked fabulous, don't you think?" Dana almost sighed.

The swing bounced crookedly as Lilith sat up. "You're kidding."

"You didn't think he was incredibly sexy?"

"No." Horror crept into her voice. "Absolutely not. If I saw him coming toward me on the street, I'd find a way to avoid him."

Dana laughed. "I'd want to be walking beside him. I'd feel safe."

"You're attracted to him!"

"What if I am?" Dana took few people into her confidence—a life in politics didn't invite much trust. She rarely talked about Randall, about their personal life, not even to her oldest friend, so why discuss Sam?

"Is he single?" Lilith asked.

"He wasn't wearing a ring."

Lilith's expression turned sympathetic. "I know you must be lonely, Dana, but there are plenty of other men who would be good choices. A man who doesn't fit into your world could cause a lot of talk. The wrong kind of talk could ruin your chances for reelection. You know that."

"I do know."

"So, you're not going to see him?"

"No."

''What are you going to do about Harley?''

The quick change of subject confused Dana. ''What about Harley?''

''He was humiliated tonight. More than once. You don't think he inherited his daddy's skill for vengeance along with the ranch?''

''He's not dealing with an ignorant seventeen-year-old this time.''

Lilith laid her hand on Dana's. ''No, he's dealing with a powerhouse. And that makes you more vulnerable than ever. Truth or lies, it doesn't matter.''

Dana pulled her hand free and shoved both fists into her robe pockets, the backs of her fingers brushing Sam's card. ''I'll be careful. I'm always careful.''

Lilith seemed about to say something but stood instead, her hand resting on her belly. ''Baby's finally gone to sleep. That's my cue.''

Five minutes later Dana went to her bedroom. The familiarity of the space that hadn't changed in all these years held a kind of comfort she hadn't felt for a long time. She stood at the open window, her long-buried needs doing battle with her longer-held sense of responsibility—to everyone but herself. She'd felt…*female* tonight. Sexy. And Sam had barely touched her.

Sam. He'd intruded in her thoughts for years and years. A question without answer. A temptation without satisfaction. Not even a kiss at the end of the prom. She'd wanted to kiss him tonight. Dancing with him, being held by him, had made her want more. A lot more.

Dana leaned her cheek against the window frame and stared at the stars. She was achingly lonely, but she wasn't in a position to do anything about it, not at this point. Nor could she tell Lilith the truth about her bid for reelection. Dana *had* made up her mind, but she couldn't make that decision public for another two months. There was too much riding on it. A promise was a promise.

As she lowered the sash to close off the night air, Dana

heard a car engine start. Headlights came on from about fifty feet up the road. A black sedan headed slowly down the hill and passed in front of her parents' house. She relaxed. Harley would drive a truck. So would his friends.

It was probably a couple of teenagers necking—she looked at the clock and saw it was 1:00 a.m.—and breaking the midnight curfew, a long tradition in Miner's Camp.

Ah, adolescence. Years ago she'd been an hour late. Her parents caught her tiptoeing into the house, and she was punished by having certain privileges taken away, like no solo dating for a month. At the time it seemed too harsh for a first offense.

In reality it had been good preparation for her public life now, where first offenses mattered enormously. She'd been careful not to make any—until now. She should've corrected Candi's statement that she was running for reelection right when it happened, no excuses, before it became the problem she expected it would become.

Because now when she made a mistake, she wasn't accountable to two loving parents but to millions of people—friend and foe. The repercussions had probably already begun.

Three

Tuesday evening Dana rested her elbows on her desk, propped her chin on her fists and studied her calendar for the rest of the month. Congress was in recess, but she was busier than ever. August was supposed to be a time to reconnect with constituents. So far, all she'd done was reconnect with the media.

She leaned back in her leather chair and closed her eyes, the hectic pace of the past few days not only catching up but hitting hard. She'd skipped the Sunday reunion picnic to head back to her San Francisco office to deal with the anticipated backlash of Candi's unfortunate misstatement, and had been home only long enough to sleep and shower since then.

In need of damage control, she'd sent for her communications director and press secretary from her Washington, D.C., office. Her chief of staff and director of state operations had apartments in San Francisco and met her at the office. More than a dozen staffers had given up their Sunday. They'd bustled in and out. Phones rang, the fax machine churned, meetings overlapped.

Sunday, Monday and Tuesday blurred into one long day. She'd been on the phone to party leaders, Senate leaders, and even her parents, who'd read the news in the Orlando newspaper before she could contact them.

The quiet of her office suddenly surrounded Dana. She'd sent everyone home, although a few still lingered, wrapping things up. She would go home herself if she could work up the energy to put on her shoes and walk to her car.

Her personal assistant, Maria Sanchez, wandered in, yawning. She smiled. "Sorry."

Dana waved off the apology. "Sleep in tomorrow. If you come in before ten I'm docking your pay."

"I will if you will."

Dana smiled at Maria's perpetual mantra. She was always trying to get Dana to take time off. "Actually I was considering going to L.A. for the day. My calendar looks like it could be cleared."

"Do you need a plane reservation?"

"I have to make a call first. I'll phone in my own reservations, thank you, Maria. And I'll let you know in time for you to postpone my meetings."

"Do you need any paperwork gathered to take along?"

"No. It's personal business."

Although curiosity lit her eyes, Maria kept her questions and comments to herself. Dana had inherited Randall's staff, and she valued each and every one of them. She'd been a staff member before her marriage four years ago and unofficially his speechwriter and strategist for the year and a half until his death.

Maria took a few steps backward. "I'll clean off my desk while you make that call." She shut the door behind her.

Dana pulled Sam's business card out of her pocket. The paper was breaking down. She really needed to stop using it like a strand of worry beads. Soon she wouldn't be able to read the print.

He'd been on her mind constantly since the reunion, and she'd been debating calling him, feeling she needed a reason. She'd finally come up with one.

She called his cell phone before she lost her nerve.

"This is Sam Remington. Please leave a message."

Voice mail. Damn. She straightened her shoulders. "Hi, Sam. It's Dana Sterling. I just learned I might have to be in L.A. tomorrow, so I thought I could drop off your medal in person. Could you give me a call, please?" She gave him her unlisted home number and the private line to her office then hung up and took a deep breath.

Exhaustion caught up with her, making her office sofa look a little too inviting. Standing, she shuffled the papers on her desk into something that resembled a stack and shoved them into her briefcase for her nightly bedtime story. She'd forgotten what it was like to curl up in bed with a good novel. Regardless, she looked forward to an evening at home.

Her private line rang. She let it ring a second time before picking it up.

"Dana Sterling."

"You're working late, Senator."

Sam. She leaned a hip against her desk and smiled, taking it as a good sign that he'd returned her call so quickly. He didn't seem surprised to hear from her. "No later than usual."

"You know what they say about all work and no play."

"You're speaking from personal experience?"

He made a sound of agreement. "I caught you on the news a few times."

"Just part of the job."

"Which is one of the reasons you're not running for a second term."

She pushed away from the desk. "I didn't say that."

"When you're bluffing, you move your left shoulder back and forth. It's harder to pick up than, say, avoiding eye contact, but it's your tell. I figured that out in tenth grade.''

He'd watched her that closely? That carefully?

She didn't answer. She couldn't. To say anything meant she would either lie or confide in him. Neither was a viable option.

"No one will hear it from me," he said into the silence. "Rumor is, by the way, that you're going to run."

She lowered herself into her chair. "Except for the press and the three men waiting to take my place, I didn't know there was such interest. Where did you hear the gossip?"

"I took an unofficial poll at a couple of watering holes on Monday."

"And the margin of error?"

"Plus or minus thirty points."

After a moment she laughed. "I suppose it'll be old news by tomorrow."

"For the general population maybe."

"It's the voters that count."

"Then I think you're safe," he said. "Politicians, on the other hand…"

"You don't have to tell me, Sam. I've been part of the process since I was twenty."

A beat passed. "Is that when you met your late husband?"

"Yes." She didn't want to discuss Randall. There had to be some rule of etiquette that said you shouldn't talk about the man you loved with the man you lusted after. "So, about the medal."

To his credit he didn't miss a beat at the change of subject. "I'll be in L.A. tomorrow, but I'm actually in San Francisco at the moment. I've got an eleven o'clock flight tonight. I could swing by your office."

He was in San Francisco and he hadn't called before now. *Not interested.* The words might as well be flashing in neon. "The medal's at home," she said coolly. "I'm headed there now. You're welcome to stop by, or I can still mail it.''

''I'll stop by.''

Really? Another mixed message. ''Okay. My address is—''

''I know where you live. See you in half an hour.''

Dana listened to the dial tone for a few seconds before cradling the phone. She liked his confidence, had always been attracted to confident men—

He knows where I live?

A quick knock on the door preceded Maria's entrance. ''About tomorrow?''

''Don't cancel my appointments. I'll go to the L.A. office next week, as planned.'' She took a final glance at her desk to see if she'd missed anything. ''Now, go home.''

''I will if you will.''

''We'll walk each other to our cars.'' Dana scooped up her briefcase and jacket then stepped into her shoes. Energy replaced exhaustion. Sam was coming.

Sam pressed the intercom button outside Dana's security gate, then pulled into her driveway when the iron gate swung open. He studied the Pacific Heights home, as he had the day before from outside the fence. She didn't live in a house but a mansion, magnificent in its grandeur but not ostentatious, the front-yard landscaping established and unfussy.

Architecture was Sam's passion. He'd looked up the history of this particular house: Mediterranean-style, built shortly after the 1906 earthquake, dominated by a red tile roof and terra-cotta colored textured stucco. The knoll-top parcel had a panoramic view from its lush rear garden of the Golden Gate Bridge, San Francisco Bay and the Presidio.

Randall Sterling had been born to money.

Sam had conducted his own research on the man when he'd first read about Dana marrying him. His rise in politics began in high school as student-body president, continued at Stanford, then went into public arenas, on committees and boards. He was voted in as congressman when he was only twenty-eight, serving twelve years before being elected to the Senate. He'd finished one six-year term and two years of a second term before dying of a massive heart attack while jogging in Golden Gate Park almost two and a half years ago.

The charismatic, beloved and respected Randall Sterling was a true man of the people. He'd earned Sam's vote. And now his widow sat in his place. No scandal had ever touched her husband or her, the only gossip the twenty-year age difference, and the fact she worked for him.

Sam had thought about her a lot through the years, had even fantasized seeing her again, but had made no effort. He hadn't been in a position to.

Now he was.

And now he couldn't.

He glanced at his watch and calculated the time until his flight. He'd allowed himself five minutes with her.

Sam set his car alarm out of habit then walked up the flagstone path to the enormous front door. He rang the bell, heard the chimes from deep within the house. He wondered whether a servant would greet him, but Dana did, looking serene in blue silk pants and blouse, which was unbuttoned one button lower than conservative. A sliver of ice-blue lace bra teased him, its texture contrasting seductively with her skin. A jolt like lightning zapped him in the midsection and turned up the heat. Fifteen years of life experience had given her a mature sexuality that appealed to him as much as her innocence had years ago.

She backed up, inviting him inside. "You look very nice in your suit and tie. Kind of Secret Serviceish."

"Secret Service men appeal to you?"

"Oh, well, actually I prefer a CIA man."

"It's that furtive look, I imagine. Makes all the women swoon."

Her eyes lit with humor as he walked past her and she shut the door. She smelled good—not flowery, but cool and tranquil. He'd bet her perfume came in a curvy blue bottle. But he missed the hot pink she always used to wear.

The tiled foyer boasted cathedral ceilings and vivid stained-glass windows, a dramatic curving staircase, textured walls painted a rich antique gold and a spectacular wrought-iron chandelier. Bold simplicity. He'd been in a lot of fancy homes in the past few years, but this one had the added element of old-world elegance, as if the furnishings had been there forever. He wondered if she'd had any hand in the decorating.

"Would you like a glass of wine, Sam? I've got a wonderful Chardonnay chilling in the living room." She gestured toward open double doors off the foyer.

He saw a flicker of candlelight, heard the strains of a classical piece he couldn't have identified if his life depended on it. She'd set a scene. *For him.*

Dammit. *Dammit.*

"I'll pass on the wine, but thanks," he said.

She looked mildly embarrassed. "Oh. You probably don't drink, do you?"

"Why wouldn't I?"

"Because of your—" She stopped, her embarrassment deepening.

He knew how the sentence ended. "Because of my father?" he asked.

"I'm sorry. I didn't mean to—"

He cut her off with a gesture. There was no faster way to change his mood than to bring up his father, but especially coming from Dana, who knew too many details of his childhood. "I drink socially. What that man did or didn't do has no bearing on who I am or how I live. I'm not drinking because I can't stay. I'm on my way to the airport."

"Already? Your flight's at eleven."

"And I have to park and go through security. You know how long that takes these days."

"Of course," she said crisply, matching his tone, making him aware of it. She walked toward the living room, giving him time to admire her backside, something he'd done too often as a teenager. When she returned she held out the medal to him.

"Thanks." He stuffed it in his pocket and turned to leave, the hardest thing he'd done in recent memory. She was a temptation beyond his expectations.

"Why'd you even bother to come?" she asked.

He glanced back. He couldn't read her expression, something between curious and hurt.

"I might as well have mailed it, you know," she said, not letting him off the hook.

I wanted to see where you live, how you live. Not from the outside, but inside, where her life wasn't open for public viewing. How could he tell her that and still play fair with her? He wished now that he'd never given her his card. He couldn't have a relationship with her. Not now. Not ever. "I thought I'd save you the trouble."

"Right. It would've been such a burden on me."

Sarcasm now. "You were the one all fired up to give it to me."

"Of course I was. You worked hard for that medal."

"Dana. It was fifteen years ago. Who cares?"

"I do." Her voice quavered; her cheeks flushed. "I liked battling with you all those years. Sure I wanted to win, to be the best, but, Sam, I was happy that if I didn't win, you did."

He felt like the biggest jerk on earth. "Dana—"

"Go on or you'll miss your plane."

He wanted to find a way to end this better. Instead he opened the door and stepped out into the night.

"Wait." She hurried toward him and grabbed his arm long enough to stop him.

"I apologize," she said. "Truly. All I can say in my

defense is that it's been a long three days. I'm exhausted, and not thinking clearly. I'm sorry I called you and made you go out of your way. I should've just mailed the medal and been done with it.''

He didn't know what to say, couldn't dare continue the conversation, not when he wanted to carry her up that sweeping staircase, find the nearest bed and bury himself in her.

''I wasn't expecting anything of you tonight,'' she said. ''Just to share a glass of wine and some conversation. Work consumes me. I wanted a little time away from it with an old friend. I didn't mean to put you on the spot.''

She sounded lonely. He understood loneliness. And because he was only human, he brushed his fingertips down her cheek, although whether for him or for her, he wasn't sure. A little sound came from her, sexier than any he'd ever heard in bed.

He walked away. She followed.

''You don't have to walk me to my car,'' he muttered over his shoulder, frustrated now.

He heard her stop walking for a second, then continue at a more leisurely pace.

''I'm getting my mail,'' she said, a little lilt to her voice.

''You get your own mail?''

''My housekeeper was off today.''

He liked the self-protective arrogance in her voice. He pushed the remote unlock button for the car. ''Nice house, by the way.''

''Nice car. Is it yours?''

''Yes.''

''You don't have to sound so defensive. You don't live in San Francisco and you're flying back to L.A. tonight. Logic says it's a rental.''

''A Mercedes?'' He climbed inside knowing he'd spend the rest of the night analyzing their conversation. ''See you, Senator.''

Moving closer to the car, she continued to eye it speculatively. "Were you… Is this what you were driving at the reunion?"

"Yes."

"You—" She stopped. "Did you guard my parents' house after the reunion, Sam?"

Distracted by the breast-level view, he hesitated a few seconds before answering. "Why would I do that?"

"Answering a question with a question doesn't work with me." She turned those dark eyes on him then, not with humor this time. "If you're leaving your car at the airport, you're coming back to the city."

"I have business here."

"When will you be back?"

"Tomorrow night." He started the car, ending the conversation, ending what might have become a relationship that mattered.

I can't be seen with you and you can't be seen with me. It's that simple.

He watched her in his rearview mirror as he pulled away. She didn't move except to cross her arms. He'd bet she was giving him hell. And damned if he didn't deserve it.

"Well," Dana said as the gate closed. "That was fun."

She heard the sarcasm in her voice, felt her face heat up and her pulse thunder.

It *had* been fun, she realized. More fun than she'd had in a long time.

People rarely argued with her anymore. Debated, yes, but nothing with fire behind it, at least not personal fire. There'd been heat between her and Sam. Lots of it. She welcomed the warmth as it settled in parts of her body she'd thought frozen.

Dana walked down the driveway to the mailbox, wondering why she bothered, except that she'd told Sam she was going to. She rarely got personal mail at home. Almost everything came to the office or was transmitted by e-mail or fax. Few people knew this address.

So how did Sam know?

Dana retrieved her Occupant mail from the box that was mounted to the iron fence and headed back to the house, resignation settling in. He'd planned his visit tonight to be short. He'd taken advantage of his flight to L.A. to stop by with a narrow time frame. If he'd wanted to spend time with her, he could have made plans to see her when he got back instead of tonight. What difference would a day or two make?

She locked the house, set the alarm, blew out the candles in the living room and grabbed the bottle of Chardonnay to return to the refrigerator.

The house seemed quieter than usual as she climbed the staircase. She no longer missed Randall's presence the way she had when he first died. She'd gotten used to coming home by herself. She hated it, but she was used to it.

She stopped in her bedroom doorway and stared at the briefcase she'd flung onto the bed, the same bed she'd shared with Randall. She hadn't changed anything, hadn't had time or interest. She felt a sudden need to redecorate, to make it hers, a lighter, airier look instead of the heavy masculine style.

She tossed the mail on top of the bed as she headed for her closet, where she changed into cotton pajamas, then climbed into bed and dragged her briefcase into her lap. Everything inside her churned.

The phone rang. She hated the hope that rose before she could tamp it down. It couldn't be Sam, and she knew it.

"Hello?"

"Hey, pal. How're you doing?"

She hid her disappointment. "Lilith, hi. I'm worn out but the worst is over. I'm pretty sure that every network and wire service has a quote by now. How are you feeling?"

"Fat."

Dana laughed, as she was supposed to, but she envied Lilith her pregnancy, her happy and full life with a husband who adored her and work that satisfied her. "This too shall pass."

"I'm an elephant. I'm sure this is month twenty-two of my pregnancy."

"You look beautiful. Jonathan undoubtedly tells you every day."

"I also look in the mirror every day. Listen, Jonathan and I would like you to come to dinner tomorrow night. Just a small group, six or eight, depending on who's available on such short notice."

"Any single men?"

"One, but it's not a setup," she rushed to add. "He's—"

"It's okay, Lilith. Really. I'm ready." She had to do something with her newly resurrected feelings, and Sam wasn't interested. A little flirtation might be a good thing.

"That's a change."

"I know. It'll be two and a half years next week. I can't survive on work alone, as much as I love it."

"Does that mean I can officially start sending men your way?"

"You mean you were telling the truth when you said tomorrow night wasn't an unofficial date?"

"Well, not exactly. But there are other men besides this one, Dana. Interesting, intelligent, emotionally secure men."

More interesting than Sam? "Okay."

"It's going to take a while for me to get used to hearing you say that. Um, I take it you didn't listen to the show today."

"I didn't have time, why?"

"Harley called in to the program."

Dana let that news sink in. Lilith hosted a Monday-through-Friday, commute-time, radio-advice show, *Dr. Lilith.* Her Ph.D. in psychology qualified her; her warm but no-nonsense personality made her a success, even though she was an ultraconservative living in a predominantly liberal city.

"Something tells me he wasn't looking for advice on his sex life," Dana said. "Although he probably needs it."

"Meow."

Dana smiled. "Did he identify himself?"

"Of course not. Coward that he is, he got on the air by telling my producer he had a question about how to help a woman lose her frigidity."

"He said that?"

"Those words exactly. I started to ask him for more specifics, when he said that surely I knew who he was talking about—the princess of Prospector High School. Anyway, I'll send over a tape to your office so you can hear it. He didn't name you, but your bio says you graduated from there."

"How'd you shut him down?"

"You'll hear the tape. Dana, I don't think he's done. His ego is black and blue, and he's an eye-for-an-eye man. Usually his money and power get him what he wants. You weren't impressed. He doesn't like that."

Lilith wasn't aware of what had happened between Dana and Harley years ago, only that they'd had a confrontation. Sam knew because he'd been involved, but Dana hadn't told anyone else except her parents, not even Randall. Like Sam, she buried bad memories.

"Thanks for the warning," Dana said. "I'll think about how to handle it."

"Good. Can you be at our house by seven tomorrow night?"

"If I can't get away that early, I'll let you know. As of now, it looks okay."

They said their goodbyes.

Dana tried to work. She needed to review two reports her staff had put together before her meetings tomorrow but her eyes kept closing. Useless, she decided. Better to get some sleep and get up an hour earlier in the morning.

She set her alarm for 4:00 a.m. then shoved her briefcase and paperwork to the other side of the bed. She would have turned out the light except that her gaze landed on an envelope sandwiched between an L.L.Bean catalog and a supermarket ad.

She slid it free. The envelope had weight and texture much like a wedding invitation, yet no return address, just her name and address, typed in a calligraphy-style font, fancy and hard to read. A San Francisco postmark. Most people addressed her mail as Senator or The Honorable. On this envelope her name bore no title of any kind, not even Ms. She opened the flap, unfolded the single sheet of cream-colored vellum.

If you run for reelection, I'll make public everything I know about your saintly *late husband.*

Four

It was 3:00 a.m. before Sam arrived at his Santa Monica home, his mood as black as the sky. First, he'd forgotten about the valedictorian medal in his pocket until he set off the airport metal detector. Then the flight was delayed over an hour because of mechanical problems. After that, the car service didn't show to pick him up and he had to take a cab home.

As he paid the driver, he counted four newspapers scattered in his driveway, even though his neighbor had promised to pick them up daily. He dragged a hand down his face. One more thing to do before he flew back to San Francisco tomorrow night—cancel the paper. He was on the road too much now, anyway.

He punched his code into the keyless entry panel then felt the cool welcome of home, his first real home, a 1920s Craftsman that suited his needs perfectly. Newly renovated and true to the original architectural style, the house had tugged at him from the first moment he saw it. The fact he could afford it still made him shake his head in wonder. The simple mission-style furniture was complemented by soothing Asian undertones and accent pieces he'd picked up in his travels. It would do until he could build the house of his dreams. He'd already designed it.

Sam detoured into his office on the way to the bedroom. The message light on his answering machine flashed. He pressed the Playback button.

"Hello, Sam, dear, it's Rosa Giannini. I'm sorry to tell you that Ernie passed away this evening. One minute he was talking to me, then he closed his eyes and he was gone.… I'm trying to convince myself he's in a better place, free of pain, but it's…hard."

Sam squeezed his eyes shut at the catch in her voice and the grief-filled pause that followed.

"The services will be on Saturday," Rosa continued. "I understand if you can't make it, though. He was so glad you came to see him last weekend. He loved you so much, Sam." She was quiet a moment, then, "You probably think he was the one doing you favors through the years, but he needed you as much as you needed him. You were a blessing in his life, in our lives. I hope you know you'll always be welcome here."

Again a pause. Sam stared at the ceiling and swallowed hard against the ache in his throat.

"Don't send flowers, dear. Do something that would make Ernie smile. You already made him proud. Stay in touch."

The scent of cherry pipe tobacco seemed to fill the room. Sam closed his eyes and saw his friend. Sweater vests and bow ties and shirts that lost their starch before the lunch bell. A fringe of salt-and-pepper hair that gave him an impish-monk look, especially when added to the Santa Claus belly. Sam heard his mentor's dry chuckle, felt a grip on his shoulder, a squeeze of encouragement.

How could he attend the funeral of the man he'd wished a thousand times was his father? How could he wear his grief openly for the person who'd made him believe in himself?

He would send flowers, though, because he'd learned that simple things helped those left behind. And for himself as well as Rosa he would do something that would make his old friend smile.

After another minute Sam's bed beckoned, singing its siren song to his weary body and soul. His training wouldn't let him go to bed without hanging up his suit and putting the rest of his clothes in the hamper. He slid under the sheets finally, closed his eyes and lay there for a few seconds before tossing the bedding aside and going to the closet. When he returned it was with his medal in hand.

He'd earned it because of Ernest Giannini, then had turned his back on the honor, which was like turning his back on his teacher, diminishing, if not discounting, its— and his—importance.

The medal meant something, Sam realized. He'd told Dana otherwise, but now he knew differently.

He gripped it hard, felt it heat his hand and the edge dig into his palm.

He needed to thank Dana for keeping the medal for him, for making him take it back. He'd not only been ungrateful but rude.

He returned to his closet and came out with a small wooden chest, which he placed on his bed. He hesitated before opening the lid, as if the contents of Pandora's box would fly out. Finally he pushed the lid up. Inside were ragged pieces of lined notebook paper torn into squares with words penciled on them, front and back. A question from him on one side, an answer from Dana on the other.

He sifted through them, remembering. Their competition to be class valedictorian had started in ninth grade when teachers began to notice how often they asked and answered questions in class. Soon they were competing for the top scores on tests and papers, encouraged by their teachers. They ran neck and neck for all four years. It had come down to the last semester. He'd gotten an A in math; she'd gotten an A minus. That was difference. The only difference.

Sam pulled a piece of paper from the box. Outside the classroom they would write questions down and slip them into each other's locker. He'd kept them all. Not just academic questions like, "What does Moby Dick represent?" but life questions and riddles and puzzles.

He looked at the one he'd grabbed.

Question: "Why did the punk rocker cross the road?"

Answer: "He was stapled to the chicken."

Sam smiled, then he remembered the one that had changed the tone of their questions. "Do you think Marsha Crandall is sexy?" she'd asked, referring to a classmate. It was the first time she'd asked a provocative question. "I told her as much just the other night," he answered, teasing, lying.

Dana had snubbed him for three days after that, but eventually it led to many more provocative questions, a flirtation on paper, although they still didn't talk outside of class much, and usually only about a project or paper. But she always looked at him expectantly, as if waiting for him to make some kind of move. He didn't have any moves to make. He wouldn't have known a move if it stood naked in front of him and waved its arms.

And now he needed to write her a note, thanking her for keeping the medal. Thank-you notes weren't his forte. He offered thanks in person, or he sent flowers or wine or something else appropriate for the favor.

What does one give the woman who has everything?

The next night Dana pulled in to her driveway after dinner at Lilith's. She'd made it through the day and evening without showing the letter to anyone. Threats were nothing new, although she'd never gotten one quite like this.

If you run for reelection, I'll make public everything I know about your saintly *late husband.*

Randall had been in the public eye all his life. What was there to tell? Why the emphasis on ''saintly''?

She should turn the note over to her chief of staff, who would make a decision about whether to take it seriously, but something stopped her. If it had been a threat to expose *her* for past deeds, she would have let the blackmailer dig. There was nothing to find, nothing shocking or newsworthy, anyway.

But this was Randall's reputation. She would guard it with her life—and her political career. Still, did one letter necessitate an investigation?

Dana felt a brush of fabric against her calves as she walked from her garage into the house. She'd gone straight from work to Lilith's after changing into something feminine and flattering at the office. The evening turned out to be lovely, her ''date'' a patent attorney, newly divorced and attentive, and entirely too agreeable. Lilith was known for throwing parties that inspired great debates long into the evening. She and her husband may be conservative, but they knew the value of cultivating people of varying convictions.

Tonight hadn't been any different, and yet it had been. The mix of people wasn't as diverse. Dana could also see that Lilith wasn't feeling well. They'd gone into her office to look at the birth announcements she'd already started designing on her computer, which was the only excuse Dana could think of for getting Lilith alone for a few minutes.

''You crafty person,'' Dana said, admiring the design. ''I don't know how you find the time.''

''When it's fun, you make the time.''

Dana settled a hand on her friend's shoulder and looked closely at her. ''You don't seem yourself tonight. Are you doing too much?''

Lilith laid a protective hand on her belly. ''Braxton Hicks,'' she said, as if Dana was supposed to know what that meant. Lilith explained that they were contractions, but not the kind indicating imminent birth, just discomfort.

Because Lilith wasn't up to par everyone agreed to make it an early evening, which was fine with Dana. The patent attorney asked if he could call her, and she'd given him her office number then headed home.

When she heard the television on in her housekeeper's room, she knocked on the door and waited. Hilda would never call out for her to enter but would come to the door, wearing her pristine white chenille robe like a suit of armor. She'd been with Randall's family forever and was in no hurry to stop working, even though she was eligible for social security and Medicare. She also believed in a strict employer/employee relationship, much to Dana's disappointment. She could have used a friendly face around the house in the months after Randall died.

"Good evening, ma'am," Hilda said.

"Hi. How were your days off with your daughter and grandchildren?"

"Fine, thank you. How was your evening at the Pauls'?"

"Very nice." *Invite me in. Let's open a bottle of wine, and talk.* "Any messages?" *Did Randall have secrets?*

"I heard your private line ring, but no one called otherwise."

Her tone wasn't hostile or condescending, but efficient. Dana stifled a sigh. "Thank you, Hilda. Good night."

Mission not accomplished, but she would keep trying. One day she'd get past Hilda's reserve.

In the foyer Dana touched the small stack of mail, hesitated, then flipped through it. Nothing but ads. She blew out a little breath before climbing the stairs. She plopped onto her bed, pushed the message button on her answering machine and began unbuttoning her dress.

"Hello, dear." Her mother. "Dad and I are having too much fun. We're staying an extra week in Orlando before we hit the road. Talk to you soon. We love you."

"Senator, it's Amanda." Her press secretary. "I need a

meeting with you first thing in the morning, if that's possible. If not, please let me know. Otherwise I'll be there at eight. Thanks.''

"Hi, Dana, this is Candi. I'm sorry to leave this on your machine but Mr. G. passed away. I knew you'd want to know. The funeral's on Saturday. Mrs. Giannini would like you to say a few words, if you plan to come. Let me know, okay?''

Dana recalled Mr. G. fondly but more as her father's friend than as a teacher. She wondered if her parents would alter their plans to be home in time for the funeral. They would have to drive their motor home straight through.

"Dana, it's Sam Remington.''

She'd just slipped her dress off her shoulders, exposing one of the new bras she'd spent her lunch hour purchasing in a rare moment of indulgence—sexy bras, panties and a couple of negligees—even though Sam had made it clear he wasn't going to contact her again.

"It's 8:10,'' he continued, his voice alone causing her body to react. Oh, she had it bad for him. "I'm at LAX, headed back to San Francisco. If you could give me a call sometime, I'd appreciate it. Thanks.''

He wanted her to call? After the way he'd left the other night? Shock fought with hope in her mind. She looked at the clock—ten-fifteen. He was probably en route, which meant she had to wait until morning to return the call.

Or, if she waited half an hour, she might catch him before he went to bed.

She got ready for bed expectantly, even looking forward to filling the time with a budget analysis for a meeting the next day. A half hour later she dragged the phone into her lap then dialed his cell number. Her skin felt prickly, her breath short.

"Sam Remington.''

"Hi, it's Dana.''

"I didn't mean you had to call tonight, Senator.''

"I'm still up working. Where are you?''

"In my car. Not far from my hotel."

"Would you rather call me back when you get there?"

"Why?"

"So that you don't have to drive and talk at the same time."

"I find that mildly insulting," he said, a smile in his voice.

She wedged her shoulders into her pillows and relaxed. "Do you know how many accidents are caused by people on cell phones?"

"How many?"

She grinned at the ceiling. "I don't remember exactly, Brainiac, but a lot."

"Get back to me with the statistics and we'll talk about it."

"I'll do that." A promise was a promise. "How was your trip?"

"Quick."

She wished he would elaborate. "Candi left a message tonight that Mr. G. died."

A beat of silence, then, "I heard."

That surprised her. "The services are on Saturday. Are you going?"

"I'm not sure."

"Oh." She'd thought they could go together. She wrapped the phone cord around her finger, wishing he would tell her why he wanted to see her, but he said nothing. "So, what was your message about? Why do you want to meet with me?"

"I have something to give you. If tomorrow after work suits you, I can stop by."

"Sure. Should I call you when I'm leaving my office? It'll be after six, I imagine, and before eight."

"That'll work."

"Sam?" she said in a hurry, afraid he would hang up. "Why did you come to the reunion?"

"To see you."

Her heart lurched. *To see me? Just to see me?* "How did you know I would be there?"

"Have you missed a reunion yet?"

His tone of voice indicated it was a rhetorical question, but she answered anyway. "No."

"Okay." Static almost covered his words. "I'm pulling in to the hotel."

She heard the line go dead. Lost reception or had he hung up? "Good night," she said, in case he could hear her.

She returned the phone to her nightstand and reached for the budget report again, forcing herself to concentrate. But when she turned out the light an hour later, she was free to think of Sam. She tried to imagine what he planned to give her but—

No. It better not be.

Before she could let a contrary voice dictate her actions, she phoned him.

"Sam Remington."

"Oh, good, you weren't asleep."

"Actually, I was."

"You sound wide awake."

"Training. What can I do for you, Blush?"

His voice softened with the question. She heard a rustle of fabric, as if he were resituating pillows. He made a sleepy kind of sound that turned her on. She considered what it would be like to be curled up next to him. She was so tired of being alone. Of handling everything alone. But it was more than that. No other man made her as deeply aware of the emptiness—and the longing.

"Dana?" he asked into the silence.

She considered his previous question. What could he do for her? You could rub my back. Hold me. Kiss me. Make love with me…. The vivid thoughts caught her by surprise. "Um, I was wondering if you'd like to come to breakfast instead."

"The suspense is killing you?"

Oh, he was enjoying this. "You'd better not be giving me the medal back."

"Or what?"

He had her there. What kind of threat could she make? She was acting like a teenager, she with her Ph.D. in political science, her position as a U.S. senator, no matter that she'd taken the fast track there. Her brains were being fried by the giddiness of infatuation, like some hormonal adolescent.

"I'm not trying to give you back the medal," he said into the long void.

"Oh." She'd been sure that was his plan. "Okay. Good. All right, then."

His laugh was low and sexy.

"So, could you come to breakfast?" she asked.

"No, but thanks for the invitation. I'll see you as planned."

"But—" She heard the click of a hang-up. Really. Did the man have something against ending conversations normally?

Well, he'd been a good sport about her waking him. She'd never done that before, called someone that late at night, unless it had been an emergency.

"What can I do for you?" he'd asked.

Even if she'd answered him honestly she doubted he would be on his way to her house. He was too independent, too strong-willed to let himself go on a whim. And, perversely, it made her want him even more.

Sam set the phone on the nightstand and rolled onto his back. Cradling his head in his hands, he tried to decide whether to smile or curse. She'd woken him up from a dream where she had the starring role. He'd survived his high-school years on those dreams, ones more dangerous now that she was a woman and even more complex, therefore more intriguing.

Even as a child she'd been unique. They hadn't been in

the same class until fifth grade, and only then because she'd skipped fourth. His mother died a month after the school year started. When he went back to class after a week, the rest of the kids wouldn't look at him, including his friends, not knowing what to say, he supposed. Even the teacher treated him differently. But Dana came up to him at recess where he stood alone against the building and told him she was sorry his mother died.

No one had used that word—died. His mother had passed away or was gone or was in heaven. He didn't know why he appreciated her directness when everyone else had talked around the painful subject, but he had. Her sympathy had made his throat ache and his eyes burn. Because of it, he'd turned away.

He also fell in love that day, had fallen for the sweet little girl with the caring eyes and tender voice. As his feelings deepened through the years, he avoided her outside of class, guarding his heart, sometimes successfully. More often not. In the end he was grateful he'd had the foresight not to say anything to her since he had nothing to offer, as her father pointed out to him the night of the prom, the one night his dreams had a chance to come true. He could not ask her out again, that point was made clear.

He'd blocked the memory for years, but he remembered now. Remembered tugging at his tie as he climbed her porch steps. Could still see her come down the stairs dressed in pink, how beautiful she looked. And she was smiling at him. Her mother and father hovering nearby, taking their picture. His awkwardness at pinning on her corsage, and her mother finally taking over. The pungent fragrance of gardenias still aroused him.

It didn't matter that he'd gotten the prom date by default when her original date broke his leg. It only mattered that she'd said yes. That she was there. That she would be dancing with him. Rosa Giannini had taught him in two days.

He could even smile now about how he'd stumbled a little the first time he'd held Dana in his arms. At the time he'd been embarrassed, but she'd kept talking as if he was the smoothest dancer in the world. She'd made him feel appreciated. Cherished. Valued.

Mr. and Mrs. Cleary chaperoned the dance. Sam was always aware of them on the sidelines, watching. When Dana went to the rest room with her girlfriends, Mr. Cleary pulled Sam aside.

"Dana has quite a future ahead of her," he said.

"Yes, sir," Sam answered, nervous about having to talk with him.

"Her mother and I don't want anything to interfere with those plans."

"No, sir. I'm sure you don't."

"I can see you care about her."

"Yes, sir."

"If you really care about her, you won't see her again after tonight."

The words hit him like a sucker punch. He should have been prepared. He would never be good enough for anyone in this town, much less Dana Cleary. His father was a drunk. He knew what people thought—the apple didn't fall far from the tree.

"I was just doing her a favor, sir," he managed to say. The evening was ruined, his dreams were shattered, and life changed. He'd barely spoken with her again, at least not until he'd come upon Harley trying to force himself on her in the woods a month later, the day before graduation. Sam wouldn't have been there in time to help her if he hadn't gone specifically to see her, violating her father's order. She never knew that, however.

Now he could see Mr. Cleary was right. Her possibilities had been endless. If something more had developed between them, he could've held her back. But the pain of her father's rejection had sucked the joy out of the evening. He had a hard time talking with her after that, and he knew she was confused by how he'd backed away. He couldn't explain it, though, without telling her what Mr. Cleary had

said. She was the lucky one. She had parents who cared
enough to make sure their daughter didn't get hurt.

An awkward end to the evening had followed. She'd
waited expectantly, but he wasn't sure if it was for a kiss.
Maybe he should have taken advantage of his one opportunity to kiss her, but he couldn't do that. It would be like
a lie. Instead, he'd stepped backward down the porch stairs,
muttering his thanks. The next day she approached him
hesitantly and said she'd had a wonderful time, but he
turned from her, leaving her to wonder what happened.

Sam rolled onto his side and pulled the sheet over his
shoulder. He'd hurt her, still she'd seemed to forgive him.
What kind of woman was that?

Five

——

Dana handled the most critical issues her staff threw at her the next morning then met privately with her chief of staff, Abe Atwater. At age sixty-two he'd been with Randall from his first days as a member of the House and had stuck with Dana during the transition and beyond. He moved like a tornado, pulling problems into the whirlwind surrounding him and spitting them back out, solved. She couldn't have survived without him. Period. He was also the only person on her staff who knew she wasn't running for reelection.

Dana passed him the threat she'd received, having finally decided she shouldn't attempt to handle it alone.

He puzzled over the note. "'If you run for reelection, I'll make public everything I know about your *saintly* late husband.' How'd you get this? It couldn't have come through this office."

"At home. In the mail. I had no idea what was inside or I would've handled it more carefully. I've probably wiped out any fingerprints that might have been there."

Abe ran a hand over his bald head. "We've come a long way from the days when people cut letters out of newspapers and magazines and glued them on a piece of paper." His smile was wry. "Computer generated, don't you think? Some fancy typeface."

"A calligraphy font," Dana said, agreeing, relaxing because he smiled. "I thought at first it was a wedding invitation. What do you think, Abe? Serious?"

"It came to your house not your office. Then there's the timing."

She nodded. "Who would've thought my nonannouncement to run would cause such a stir. Obviously someone doesn't want me to be reelected, but what could they have on Randall?"

"Nothing that I know of." He paced her office, staring at the piece of paper as if something else would appear on it.

"Are you sure?" she asked. "Doesn't everyone have something in their past they wouldn't want revealed?"

"Do you, Senator?"

"Nothing morally reprehensible, but certainly embarrassing things I wouldn't want everyone to know. How do I protect Randall's reputation when he's not here to counter any accusation?"

He rubbed his chin. "I don't think we can turn this over to the staff, much as I'd like to."

"Why not?"

"Because I have a sense that it will need to be handled privately and quietly. The fewer people involved, the better." He snapped his fingers. "That P.I. whose card was on your desk, Remington? What do you know about him?"

She didn't even have to think about it. "That I don't want to use him."

"Why not?"

Why not, indeed? It wasn't that she didn't trust Sam. He knew in high school how to keep his mouth shut, and she assumed he hadn't changed in that regard. But what if the threat had teeth? What if there was something in Randall's past? Politics were a dirty business, with surprising and often devastating consequences. What if she was inadvertently putting Sam or his reputation at risk?

She refused to be responsible for something happening to him *again* because of her. Anyone willing to smear a dead man's reputation wouldn't hesitate to ruin someone else's.

"Senator?"

Dana picked up a pen as if getting back to work. "See what you can find out on your own first, please. Sam's a friend. I'd rather not involve him."

"I'm not sure I know where to start."

"I have faith in you." She smiled at him. "You can do anything."

"Including finding a needle in a haystack?" He walked toward the door, taking the letter with him. "I'll see what I can do."

Dana left the problem in his competent hands and got back to work.

Sam stood at a window of his hotel suite, more curious than he'd been in a long time. He glanced at his watch—almost 5:00 p.m. An hour ago he'd gotten a call on his cell phone from Abe Atwater, Dana's chief of staff, asking for a meeting. A private meeting. Echoes of her father taking him aside at the prom had reverberated in his mind first, followed by the self-admonition that he wasn't that teenager anymore, that he was a successful adult, equal to Dana in every way.

Still, what could her chief of staff want with him?

The knock on the door heralded an end to his question. Sam greeted the immaculately dressed man, inviting him into the sitting area of the suite before taking a seat across from him.

"What can I do for you, Mr. Atwater?"

"I assume everything we discuss will be in confidence?"

Sam resented the start of the conversation. No one questioned his integrity. No one. And if this man intended to warn him off Dana... "You're not a client," Sam said.

"I hope to be." Abe leaned forward. "I didn't mean to insult you. I wouldn't be here if I didn't already trust you, based on what I've learned."

Sam relaxed his hands and nodded.

Abe passed him a plastic bag containing a sheet of heavy paper. "Dana received this at her home night before last."

Sam read the note. Night before last? He'd been at her house night before last. She'd intended to go to her mailbox after he pulled away, must've gotten it then. "What does it mean?" Sam asked.

"If I knew, I wouldn't be here."

"You want me to find out?"

"Yes. We need to keep this under wraps, obviously. I'd rather not involve anyone else on staff until we know what we're dealing with."

Sam turned the bag over and examined the envelope. San Francisco postmark. "Is that why you came here instead of having me go to Dana's office?"

"Dana doesn't know I'm here."

Sam lifted his gaze sharply to Abe's. Dana hadn't asked for him? "Then how do you know about me?"

"I saw your business card on her desk yesterday and asked about it, although I've known about you for a couple of years. She said you were a friend. You're good. You're discreet. You get the job done."

"I'm in San Francisco because I'm already working a case." Sam passed the note back to Abe. "I can't take the job."

"Why not?"

"There's too little information to go on for a quick resolution." More important, Dana hadn't asked for him. Didn't have faith in him. Why should he help? "I can recommend someone."

"No, thanks." Abe stood, irritation evident in his posture. "I have other sources. I thought because you were her friend…" The sentence trailed off. "My mistake."

Sam shut the door after him and returned to the window. The view of the city barely registered. He'd earned the trust of countless people, people of higher rank than Dana. People who didn't doubt his abilities.

How could he go to her house now and act as if he didn't know she didn't trust him?

Sam made his decision to finish what he'd started, which meant meeting Dana when she called so that he could thank her properly for returning his medal. He hadn't gotten where he was by backing down from tough decisions or situations.

He arrived at her house ahead of her. Knowing she'd be along momentarily, he sat in his car, his engine idling, and glanced at the box on the passenger seat. A rare lack of confidence slithered through him. Any gift he usually gave was wrapped at the store and delivered. He'd wrapped this one himself, and it showed. Simple rice paper and twine, nothing fancy. There was no note because he'd had no idea how to balance the meaning of the gift with his desire to keep his distance. Although, keeping his distance had gotten easier, thanks to Abe Atwater's visit.

In his rearview mirror he spotted her white Lincoln approaching. She waved as she passed by, and he followed her through the gate then met her at the garage.

Her face lit up when she greeted him. A fierce and uncontrolled longing roared through him. He was no longer bound by any promises, but Dana Sterling was untouchable in a different way now, more for his sake than hers this time. Plus, there was the new issue between them.

"Hi, honey, I'm home," she said, a sparkle in her eyes. "What's for dinner?"

She laughed, the sound pure magic, then reached for his hand and started walking toward a back courtyard encircled by a lush garden. He let her take him along, deciding to share the moment as he might have had he not known she didn't have faith in him as an investigator.

"Let's sit outside. It's such a beautiful evening," she said.

Her skin felt good, soft and smooth. She brought her body a little closer, enough that he became aware of her perfume. He closed his hand around hers a little more tightly.

Her steps slowed. She didn't say a word, although he caught her eyeing his gift. When they reached a cushioned swing big enough for two, she slipped her hand from his and sat just to the right of middle.

He sat beside her, setting the package in her lap. Her hands shook as she curved her fingers over the box, keeping it from falling. Nerves? Over him? He didn't know how he felt about that.

Or was she thinking about the threat?

"You can open it," he said when she made no attempt to do so.

"I'm practicing self-control."

"What, you usually tear into a package?"

She shook her head but didn't explain. She toyed with the twine. Finally she unwrapped the box without tearing the delicate paper, lifted the lid and peeled back the bubble wrap and tissue paper. "Oh! It's beautiful. Breathtaking. It's a Japanese Noh mask, isn't it?"

"Zo-onna, she's called. She represents calmness and purity. This one is a century old."

"A century… Imagine." She ran her fingers over the beautifully carved face, tracing the features. She met his gaze. "She's exquisite, truly, Sam, but I couldn't possibly accept it."

"I would've thought you would know how to accept a present. You say thank-you. And that's all you say."

"But I didn't do anything to warrant this spectacular gift."

He angled toward her, sliding his arm along the back of

the swing. "I finally realized what the medal meant. Thank you."

Her eyes seemed to see so far into his soul he almost couldn't breathe. Her lips curved into a soft smile. "You're welcome."

The simplicity of her words and the open pleasure on her face warmed him, making him ignore the hurt she'd caused. She held the mask to her chest and sat back, bringing her shoulder in contact with his hand. Everything stilled—the insects, the birds, the air. She looked at him with such need....

From the corner of his eye he caught a movement, then saw a gray-haired woman carrying a tray, walking along the flagstone path.

Dana leaned toward him, her voice low. "You're not getting away so fast tonight. I asked my housekeeper to bring some wine and hors d'oeuvres. You'll stay, won't you?"

"It seems to be an executive order."

"What good is power if you don't use it?" she asked sweetly, even though they both knew it hadn't been an order and he certainly wasn't obligated to accept.

"Thank you, Hilda," she said as the woman set the tray on a table in front of the swing. "This is Sam Remington."

"Mr. Remington."

Starched, he decided. Or she hated him on sight. "The food looks great."

She nodded.

He watched her march back to the house. "She could take on a few drill sergeants I know."

"I'd like to say that under that surface lurks a heart of gold, but I haven't seen it. She's the most consistent person I know, however. You're the first man I've had to the house, so she's a little curious."

"You haven't dated?"

She busied herself with the wine. He came to his own conclusion.

"Why not, Dana?"

"Oh, time. Energy. Interest. The fishbowl. You know."

He was reading between the lines and purposefully kept his voice gentle. "We can't date, you know."

"I know." She lifted her head. "Why can't we?"

He almost smiled. She used to question everything. He'd liked that. He still liked it, even though he didn't really want her to be so appealing.

"That fishbowl you mentioned," he told her, taking the wine bottle from her to pour. He passed her a glass and gave her the only reason out of several complicated ones he thought she would believe. "You're public and I'm private. Anonymity is critical to my job."

"I checked you out." She looked at him over the rim of her wineglass.

"I expected nothing less. What'd you find out?"

"That you're the R in ARC Security & Investigations, a private-investigation firm not listed in the Yellow Pages. From what I can tell, you work by referral only and take only high-profile cases. Politicians, celebrities, business executives and the wealthy in general. Your reputation is impeccable. Yours and the firm's."

Yet you don't trust me?

She sipped her wine. "But as far as anonymity goes, Sam, you don't exactly blend into the background, you know."

"Are you flattering me? I can become as invisible as I need to be."

"Not when there are women around."

He didn't have an answer to that compliment, so he let it go.

"Although you scare Lilith," she said.

"Well, you know those conservatives. Afraid of their own shadows."

They drank Chardonnay and ate an entire platter of antipasto—tangy marinated green olives, a mellow cheese he didn't recognize, paper-thin slices of prosciutto, and bruschetta piled with diced tomato and drizzled with olive oil.

"How did you end up in the army?" she asked.

His gaze was drawn to a drop of oil glistening at the corner of her mouth. Thoughts of the ways he could remove it had his imagination working overtime, but he picked up his wine instead. "My car broke down in front of an army recruiting office. The recruiter bought me breakfast and talked me into enlisting, said I'd have plenty of money for college when I got out. I stayed in for eight years."

"Did you go to college?"

"No." He hadn't even regretted it.

She eyed the tray, then picked up an olive. "Why did you leave home so fast?"

"You of all people should know the answer to that. There was no reason to stay." *My father was a drunk. Your parents didn't want me near you. And you—you wouldn't even look at me at graduation.* Any one of those reasons would have been enough. Instead, he'd had all three.

"I'm sorry you got hurt." She laid a hand on his. "There's something you should know."

He didn't want to hear any more about the past. And now the present was getting complicated. "Look, Dana, it's over and done as far as I'm concerned. End of a very old chapter." She was asking too many questions. He had a few of his own. Instead, he made a point of looking at his watch then set his wineglass on the tray. "I need to go."

"Sam?"

He froze as he felt her hand against his back. "What?"

"This is it, isn't it?"

"It?"

"The end of the road. You won't contact me again."

He finally sat back and looked at her. "The stakes are too high. For both of us."

"Why?"

"I'm the invisible partner in my firm, and I like it that

way. And you're one of the most eligible women in the state. People are watching you.''

''You're saying we can't date because it could hurt your career?''

''Yes.'' Among other reasons. ''And yours, too.''

Her gaze was steady, the pause long. ''Then, you owe me a kiss.''

He didn't pretend not to understand. She was referring to the night of the prom when he'd left her at her doorstep without even a handshake. He'd ached to kiss her. Had hungered for it for so long he thought he might die of it. He had no reason not to kiss her now.

He slipped his hand under her hair and along her neck, drawing her forward. He hesitated even when he didn't want to. He shouldn't do this. It could only cause problems—

''Don't think,'' she said, soft and urgent, reading his mind. ''Just do.''

It wasn't only her command that made him close the gap but the fulfillment of a dream.

Her lips quivered beneath his, then went lax when he pressed a little harder. Ah, but she tasted good, smelled good, felt good. She flattened a hand to his chest, made a sexy little sound as she brought herself closer. He deepened the contact, savoring her. A Chardonnay kiss, full-bodied, crisp, intoxicating. The actuality matched his every fantasy. He felt her lean into him, felt her hands slip around his neck, bringing herself closer.

Electricity shot through him, surging farther and faster by the second, overloading his system…

He had to break the contact. He forced himself to pull back. She let her hands slide down his shoulders and re-settle on his chest, keeping the connection, the delicate contact arousing him even more. Her eyes were still closed. If he hadn't looked away to break the spell, he wouldn't have seen the shadowy figure at the window, watching them.

Hilda. She stepped back instantly. It cooled Sam faster than a loaded gun pointed to his head.

"Are you sure this can't go any further?" Dana asked, trailing a finger down his tie, finally opening her eyes.

He caught her hand. "I'm sure."

"How about if we just sleep together?" She looked surprised at her own words.

Stop fueling my dreams. "You deserve more than that. Too much secrecy for you."

"I don't care."

"Yes, you do. Or you would, anyway."

"You can't dictate my feelings," she muttered, standing.

He stood, too. "I need to go."

He saw her irritation in the way she picked up the tray, which made her fumble the mask tucked under her arm.

"I'll carry the tray inside," he said, reaching for it.

"Oh, you don't need—okay, okay." She reboxed the mask, took a final sip of wine then pointed to a back door. "It leads to the kitchen."

There was no sign of Hilda as they made their way through the house to the foyer. He saw a small stack of mail on a chest. She'd arrived at the house with him, so she hadn't seen her mail yet. He tried to determine if one of the envelopes matched the one Abe had shown him, but he couldn't tell without thumbing through them.

In his experience the more specific the threat, the more likely it was to be followed through. This one was specific.

Talk to me, Dana. Tell me about the threat. Trust me.

But she didn't say anything, just looked at him with an expression he couldn't read. Hell. He wanted to kiss her again. Hold her against him. Help her. Old habits were hard to break, even after a fifteen-year interruption.

"Goodbye, Dana," he said, turning to leave.

"Bye." A single word uttered with a slight hitch.

He ignored the way it made his gut clench and kept walking.

His mood was foul when he got back to his hotel. Twenty minutes later his cell phone rang.

"Mr. Remington, it's Abe Atwater. She got a second letter tonight."

He mouthed a curse. "What was in it?"

"A veiled threat this time. 'I'm waiting for your press conference. I won't wait long.'"

"What did Dana say?"

"She's upset, of course. Her husband's reputation means a great deal to her."

Her husband. Sam tended to forget about him. "I'll call her. But unless she asks me, I'm not getting involved in the investigation."

"That's fair. You'll let me know?"

"Yes." Sam cut him off then dialed Dana.

She answered on the third ring. "Hello?"

"You said earlier there was something I should know," he said, keeping his voice businesslike. "I cut you off. What did you want to tell me?"

Six

Dana welcomed the opportunity to explain what she'd tried to tell him. She sat on her bed. Her gaze landed on the note she'd just received. "It's about our graduation ceremony."

"When you wouldn't talk to me?"

Sam's words sliced into her, the pain still fresh after all these years. Until now she could only guess how hurt he'd been. "Harley told me if I even looked at you, he and his friends would make sure you wouldn't walk again."

His silence ratcheted up her anxiety a notch. Finally he said, "You were protecting me?"

"Of course I was protecting you. Why does that seem ridiculous? You'd rescued me from Harley," she said, bringing the issue into the open. "Then when you told me not to tell the police, I did. And you were beaten up because of it. How could I possibly take the chance that something else would happen to you? How could I live with that?"

"So instead you made me think you hated me?"

Dana looked blindly around her bedroom. A chill came

over her, whispering along her skin, raising her flesh in goose bumps. "I did what I had to do."

"I thought you were stronger than that, Dana. Even then."

The accusation in his voice startled her. "Meaning what?"

"If Harley had followed through on the threat, you could've testified. I was safe. Or did you think he would hurt you, too?"

"I didn't think. I was scared."

"You should've trusted me. Believed in me."

Dana caught her breath at the intensity in his voice, which seemed to say so much more than the words themselves. "I'm sorry," she said.

Again she was met with silence, as if he was waiting for more.

"I don't know what else to say, Sam."

"Then I guess that says it all." He hung up without saying goodbye.

Dana fell back on the bed and closed her eyes. What did he want? For her to go back and change history? She would if she could. He was seeing the experience through adult eyes. They were teenagers then, without much life experience. She'd believed in the legal system. She thought if she reported Harley for attempted rape he would be punished. Sam had known better, had tried to convince her of it. He'd asked her not to involve the police, but she had anyway, thinking he was wrong. She'd been so naive. Harley's rich daddy had taken care of everything. And Harley and his friends had taken care of Sam.

Her fault. All her fault. She'd lived with the guilt ever since.

She rolled onto her side, tucked her hands under her cheek and stared at the telephone. He'd been making a point on the phone—that he was trustworthy. That he'd wanted her to believe in him—then and now, she realized. Was she wrong not to confide in him about the letters she'd received? But what if something happened—again—because of her? This time to his hard-earned reputation.

You should've trusted me. Believed in me.

His words echoed. She sat up and dangled her legs over the side of the bed, her gaze fixed on the carpet. Finally she picked up the phone and dialed. Her hands shook. She put her head back, lifted her chin and swallowed.

"Sam Remington."

"I need your help."

A long pause, then, "Dana?"

"Yes." She found strength in knowing he was there. "I've gotten a couple of notes in the mail. I—"

"Don't say anything else. I'll be there in fifteen minutes."

He hung up. She swallowed the burn in her throat. Then she changed into sweatpants and a T-shirt and waited for him.

Dana opened the front door as he walked from his car. He wore jeans and a white shirt, the long sleeves rolled up a few turns. His leather jacket was slung over his shoulder. She wanted to burrow into him.

"Where's Hilda?" he asked, low, when he stopped close to her.

"In her room."

"Where can we go so we're sure not to be overheard?"

Dana considered it. "There's a sitting room off of my bedroom. But Hilda wouldn't—"

"Take me there."

She led the way up the staircase. He seemed to have taken on height and weight yet moved so quietly she couldn't hear his footsteps, even though he wore boots, and she had to turn twice to make sure he was there.

She was fascinated by how he'd taken charge instantly and could move soundlessly.

When she stopped to grab the note from her bed she saw him make a quick survey of her bedroom, then they went into the adjoining sitting room, her private refuge. He sat in a wingback chair. She took a seat on the blue toile sofa and tucked her feet under her. She passed him the note.

"The first one came on Tuesday. It said—"

"I know the contents," he said, examining the paper in the plastic bag.

It wasn't at all what she'd expected. "How?"

He met her gaze. "Your chief of staff came to see me today. Then he called me tonight about the second note."

"I specifically told Abe not to contact you."

"That's between the two of you." He leaned forward. "What's your take on the situation?"

Dana was still trying to digest the fact he'd already known about the note when he'd been here before. He hadn't let on at all. He hadn't even asked her why she hadn't told him about it.

"I don't know what to make of it," she said. "In fact, I almost thought the first one was a hoax. My office gets threats on occasion. They never amount to anything."

"These came to your home."

She hesitated. "Yes."

"You took precautions to preserve evidence this time?" he asked.

"I did."

"You have no theories about who's behind it?"

"None."

"Do you think there's truth to it? That your late husband had a secret?"

He'd voiced her fear out loud. "He was a good man, Sam. The best. I know it. I believe it. I don't believe Randall had anything to hide, but…"

"But how would you know for sure?"

She nodded. "Look, I get hate mail like any other politician, and my staff handles that. This is different. This is personal. I won't allow anyone to tarnish Randall's legacy. He's not here to defend himself, so it's up to me."

"Again, I remind you that these letters came to your

home, not your office, which puts a different spin on things. Even though there's no death threat, it's a threat, nonetheless."

"Who can I trust? This is a stab at me more than Randall."

"Why don't you just announce now you're not running?"

"Because then the blackmailer wins. And—I'm trusting you with this part—the party leaders asked me not to announce yet."

"Asked or told?"

She waved a hand. "Both, I suppose, but I'm respecting their wishes. We know who'll run if I don't. He's divisive, and the party needs cohesion. The opposition will be particularly strong without an incumbent to run against. We need our guy in place first, with my full support as well as the party leaders'. As long as everyone thinks I'm running, we keep a level of control. And the longer we wait, the shorter the time for others to campaign."

"Can't the process be speeded up?"

"I don't know what time frame I'm working within, but the notes seem to indicate I don't have much time at all. Plus, the party leaders would need to know why I wanted to push things up by two months," she said, noticing he hadn't moved since she'd started talking but rested his arms on his thighs and never took his eyes off her.

"Sam, Randall was forty-eight years old when we married. He'd lived a life already. If he had secrets, they stayed secret. He seemed genuine, but how can I be sure?"

"Do you want to call Abe and include him in this discussion? He may know something he doesn't realize he knows."

She smiled, grateful she could. "That actually made sense to me. No. He wasn't happy about being given the task."

"All right. Let's start at the beginning."

* * *

Sam finally sat back and looked at the room they had shared for an hour. Her bedroom was clearly Mediterranean-style—dark wood, the same antique-gold walls as the foyer, heavy drapes and ornate architectural details. But the sitting room was blue. Light. Feminine. Dana.

He'd sent her for a snack because he needed a few minutes alone to sort through what she'd told him. He ran down the facts in his head. She'd met then-Congressman Randall Sterling when she was a junior at UC Berkeley and he was a guest lecturer. Believing in his platform and his ideals, she worked on his campaign for Senate. After he won she volunteered and interned in his San Francisco office while she earned her B.A. in political science then became a paid staff member during the six years it took to get her master's and Ph.D. She married the senator the same month she finished her studies, and he died a year and a half later.

She said they hadn't been more than friendly until three months before their marriage, when they suddenly took a different kind of notice of each other.

It was obvious she'd loved, respected and admired him.

Sam didn't think the marriage was a political move on Randall's part. He was in his second term, having won by a landslide. His marriage to Dana was his first, but Sam couldn't get a handle on whether it was a passionate relationship as well as a comfortable one. He was going to have to press the point if she expected him to see what potential source of blackmail existed—or if it was an empty threat. She wasn't going to like it.

He wandered around Dana's sitting room, picking up a framed photo here and there—her parents; Lilith's wedding picture; an invitation to a party thrown by Lilith to celebrate Dana's Senate victory; Dana with Lilith, Candi and Willow when they were about sixteen, grinning, arms wrapped around each other like teenage girls do. The picture made him smile, too. Beside it was a small photo of Dana with her husband in some tropical paradise, leis around their necks.

Their quick, private wedding had been cause for speculation. Sam had followed the story more than he cared to admit, but when she didn't turn out to be pregnant, and Randall's staff all expressed how much they liked and respected Dana, the talk stopped.

Sam returned the picture to its place. They were an attractive couple, well matched and physically fit. In the photo they were smiling at each other but she wasn't leaning into him. He wasn't touching her. If this was their honeymoon...

Jealousy slammed into him even as Sam tried to convince himself he had no right to feel it. He'd forfeited his chance by not seeking her out when he left the army and returned to California. He'd made it a point to find out where she was living and what she was doing, but he'd left it at that.

Now he regretted kissing her earlier, even though he'd believed he would never see her again. Even though he'd wanted to take that memory with him. The intimacy brought an element to their relationship that interfered with the business at hand, especially considering how personal he was about to get with her.

He turned away from the bookshelf with all its photos and spotted a wide-mouthed ceramic urn on a side table, the cork top sitting upside down on the tabletop. He peered inside. His stomach clenched. The notes. She'd saved the notes. And she'd been looking at them, as he had been.

He heard Dana come into the bedroom and moved to take the tray from her when she came through the doorway.

"I got the evil eye from Hilda," she said, looking much more relaxed than when she left. Obviously she'd needed a break, too. "She doesn't like me messing around in her kitchen." She sighed. "I don't think I'll ever get used to having a servant."

"You think you could do the job you do without help at home?"

"No. But I wish I could."

"What about in D.C.?" He sat on the sofa, close to the coffee table where he'd placed the tray, then he dipped a chicken strip into a red sauce.

"I have a cleaning service, but that's all. I eat out most of the time. Meetings often run well into the night."

He took a bite and nodded his appreciation for the food. "I've heard the women senators meet for dinner once a month."

"That's true. They took me under their wing the day I arrived. We may not agree on everything, but we respect each other, and they've been generous." She snatched a stalk of cold asparagus from the tray then kicked off her shoes and joined him on the sofa, sitting cross-legged.

Her T-shirt clung even more tightly when she moved. He liked watching her. She had a graceful way about her that he associated more with women who lived leisurely lives, not someone with Dana's work ethic.

"I hope iced tea is okay," she said, leaning to pour two glasses.

By unspoken agreement they finished eating before they continued their discussion. Finally she wadded her napkin and tossed it onto the empty tray. "I needed that," she said, rearranging pillows on the sofa and nestling into them. "Let's keep going."

He picked up where they left off. "Two things. First, we need a motive. That's key. Second, dig into Randall's background."

"How will you check out his background?"

He was more concerned with figuring out who was after Dana than about Randall's past, but she couldn't seem to set aside her concern. "Interviews, for one."

She started shaking her head.

"No choice, Dana. I'm sure we'll need to talk to his

oldest friends and staff members, people who would keep his secrets, if he had them.''

''What if one of them is the blackmailer?''

''Then interviewing them will be even more helpful. There isn't any other way to determine who Randall's enemies were. Who had grudges? What about former employees? An ex-lover jealous of you? Only personal contact can yield that kind of information.''

''It seems like Abe would be the one to know. And he says he doesn't.''

''Surely Randall had other friends?''

''Of course, but politics were his life. Let me think on it. What else will you do?''

''See what we can get off the envelope aside from the San Francisco postmark. DNA and fingerprints, if we can.''

''You can get DNA from the envelope?''

''If they licked the flap. Short-term, we might get gender and race. We can use what we get toward either eliminating someone or making them a strong possibility. If we had more time, who knows? Next step, an assets search, personal and professional finances, including campaign contributions. I'll get my partners up here tomorrow to run that side of it. That'll free me for the interviews.''

She paled. ''How many people are going to be involved?''

''Dana, if I didn't trust my partners one hundred percent, I wouldn't involve them. If we don't keep confidences, we don't stay in business.''

''I expect you to use an alias for your written records.''

He thought she was being unnecessarily paranoid but didn't say so. ''Okay. As for motive—what harm is caused by revealing something about Randall's past? His reputation would be soiled. So what?''

''What do you mean, 'so what?' He spent his life—''

''Bad choice of words. I apologize. What I mean is, who is most affected by revealing his secrets? You.''

''Well, I figured that out.''

He liked when she got short with him because it meant she'd let her guard down, reminding him of the girl she'd been. If they'd had a different kind of relationship he would've teased her about it. "Give me some possibilities."

"Someone who wants my seat in the Senate."

"Someone from either party."

She nodded. "Or not even the candidate but someone who wants him in office. It could be done without his knowledge or agreement."

"That's potentially a big number."

"Could be, yes." She rubbed her temples.

"What other possibilities?"

"Someone who plain old doesn't want *me* to win."

"Anyone come to mind?"

"No."

"I can think of one."

She looked puzzled.

"Harley Bonner," he said.

"Harley's not smart enough. What could he have on Randall?"

"Harley's rich enough to hire smart. And we don't know what anyone could have on Randall, do we?" He sipped his iced tea. "Hilda?"

Dana's eyes widened. She laughed. "You're kidding."

"Until you've ruled someone out, keep them on the list. Did she resent you marrying Randall?"

"I have no idea. She doesn't show emotion of any sort, like or dislike."

"You said she gave you the evil eye in the kitchen. She also saw us kiss."

He said nothing as Dana absorbed that information then levered herself off the sofa. She wandered to the window overlooking the backyard, her arms crossed.

"The motive may not even involve you, Dana, except as a barrier to someone else's goals. I'm pointing out possibilities."

"Okay." She traced a square on the windowpane. "What else?"

"Could Randall have had an affair? A child out of wedlock?"

"He wouldn't have turned his back on a child. As for an affair, he had no reason to have one."

A spiraling path of jealousy once again swept through Sam and wouldn't dissipate. "People stray for lots of reasons."

"Our sex life was fine," she said, an edge to her voice. "Good."

"Not great?"

She faced him.

"You were married a year and a half," he pointed out, making himself treat her like any other client. "You were still on your honeymoon. Sex should've been great."

"I had no complaints."

"Did you have comparisons?"

Her jaw got tighter. "Yes."

He hesitated, then came close. He almost put his hands on her shoulders. "I have so little information to work with. I know it's hard to tell me."

"Especially you." The words seemed to stick in her throat.

"Why?"

"Because you already saw me at my worst."

An image flashed. Dana, her blouse torn away, skirt pushed up, her body covered by Harley's holding her down. She bucked beneath him, giving her all to get away. He had one hand on her mouth, the other trying to unzip himself. Sam had grabbed him by the shirt, yanked him off and threw him aside like a sack of garbage, finding a strength he didn't know he had.

After he'd chased Harley off, he turned to Dana. The shell-shocked look in her eyes ripped through his soul. She'd sat there, not moving, not attempting to gather the tattered remains of her blouse. He'd taken off his shirt and draped it around her, helping her slip her arms into the sleeves, but otherwise not touching her.

"What happened before wasn't your fault," he said. "Neither is this."

She shrugged. "Randall and I had everything in common. We thought alike. We believed in the same principles. I felt useful. I was happy."

"But?"

She stopped him with a look. "Sex isn't everything, you know."

That brought him up short. The passion in her dark eyes made him push when caution dictated restraint. "No?"

"Absolutely not."

"What *is* everything?"

She made a sweeping gesture with her hand. "Common goals and values. Supporting each other through good times and bad. Knowing what to expect at—"

"Were there bad times?"

She looked confused at the interruption. "Well, no. Not yet. But we would've supported each other."

"And that was enough to make you happy?"

"What do you want to hear? That I wanted to swing from the chandelier?"

"Did you?"

"Gymnastics don't— Dammit, Sam. I haven't lived a sheltered life. I've read the *Kama Sutra*."

"Ah."

He could see by her expression that she finally understood he was trying to lighten the moment. "I'm trying to figure out if Randall cheated on you," he said. "And if it's come back to haunt. You really don't think there was another woman?"

"No." She glared at him. "Not a man, either."

"I keep going back to the word *saintly*. It implies something personal. And moral."

"If I knew I would tell you."

He realized she'd reached the end of her tolerance for

the interrogation. He scooped up his jacket. "You'll need to get Hilda out of the house tomorrow."

Several seconds passed before she showed signs of having heard him. Exhaustion stole over her face. Ah, Dana. Show me anything but vulnerability.

"Why?" she asked.

"I need to check out the house."

"For what?"

"Clues. I'm assuming he had an office here."

"Yes. I've never noticed anything out of the ordinary, though."

"You weren't looking."

"Okay. I'll figure out something. Sam—" She touched his arm. "Thank you."

"We'll get to the bottom of it, I promise you. Get some sleep. Call me when Hilda's gone. You can stay home tomorrow, right?"

"It'll take a little finagling, but yes."

"Can you ask Abe to come here?"

"Sure."

"I'll need the names and addresses of your attorney and accountant."

"Okay."

"I'll let myself out." He wanted to hold her, to rub her shoulders until she stopped holding them so stiffly. "Good night."

She tried to smile. The effort twisted his stomach into a tighter knot.

He eyed her bed as he left the room, wishing he weren't picturing her there with her husband. Wishing, too, that he'd asked her why she'd told Abe not to contact him about her letters. But that opportunity was gone.

He walked down the hallway and descended the stairs, observing the house differently than when they'd climbed the stairs earlier. She fit here. Her father had been right all those years ago. Perhaps she'd achieved even more than he'd expected. The road she'd taken had led to a life of helping others, of doing good, of leaving a legacy when she was done.

She truly had been destined for something better than Sam could have offered her then. Here was the proof.

Seven

Late the next afternoon Dana sank into a chair in front of Randall's desk in the downstairs office. Seeing Sam seated behind the monstrosity wasn't as odd as she'd anticipated. He was big enough to do it justice.

She wanted to touch him, she realized with a jolt. To march over to him and kiss him senseless.

"Anything new?" she asked, forcing herself to be businesslike.

He sat back, the chair squeaking a little. "Not much. I've been through every file and searched all the bookshelves. I was just about to start checking out the other rooms." He pointed to a large piece of paper spread out on a table, the curling ends weighted with books. "I even found a copy of the original house design. So, how'd it go in the attic?"

"I pulled a couple of boxes you might want to look at. Mostly it's old furniture, and clothing that would sell for plenty in the vintage market. Nate said to tell you that everything's in order, so far.'' She liked his partners. Nate Caldwell, Southern California blond and handsome, was a nice foil to Arianna Alvarado's dark beauty. She was no dainty lady, but a no-nonsense, I-can-take-care-of-the-world woman. Sam had already interviewed Randall's attorney and accountant, then brought boxes of paperwork to the house with him before his friends arrived that morning. They'd gone right to work in the library. Sam had settled in the office next door after lunch.

"How long have you known Nate and Arianna?" she asked.

"Since just after boot camp."

"Were you in the same unit?"

"We worked the same details off and on." He rapped his knuckles on the table. "I have a feeling we're not going to find an answer here," he said, changing the subject. "If anything tangible existed, I doubt it was something he'd keep to be discovered later."

"He wouldn't have expected to die so young."

"True. But he would be aware of potential damage. If it's something personal enough to destroy his 'saintly' reputation, there might not be physical evidence."

She'd come to the same conclusion. "Meaning it may come down to someone making an accusation that no one can confirm or deny."

"I'm afraid so."

How could she fight that? There had to be another angle, she just hadn't thought of it yet. "Hilda should be back soon, Sam."

He looked at his watch. "We can't quit now," he said, "so I suppose we need to come up with a reason why we're all here. I expect we'll be at this well into the night."

"I don't need to tell her anything other than we're working. Should I ask her to fix dinner for all of us?"

"That'd be good, thanks." He moved to the table where the house plans lay and leaned on his palms to study the page. He shifted his shoulders as if to loosen the muscles.

Dana took a chance. She came up behind him, put her hands on his shoulders and pressed hard with her fingers. His body went rigid.

"Don't pull away," she said. "You've done so much for me."

He relaxed his shoulders by degrees. She liked that he didn't argue, even though she'd found that she liked arguing with him. As tired as she'd been last night, she hadn't been able to sleep, and it wasn't for worrying about Randall or the threat. She'd held her fingers to her lips, trying to recapture the kiss.

"Did you sleep last night?" she asked, continuing the massage, enjoying it probably more than he, as she filled her own need to touch him.

"Some." He arched a little as she pressed along his spine, moving lower, then heading back up before he stopped her for venturing too low. He never stopped studying the house plans.

"You could lie down for an hour now," she said.

"I don't nap."

She smiled at his words, as if he'd been insulted. Then an involuntary sound came from him as her thumb hit a spot along his shoulder blade.

She worked at it, felt the knot smooth out. He had an amazing body, the ideal male with broad shoulders and chest, narrow waist and hips. Beautiful. She wanted to lay her head against his back, wrap her arms around him—

He jerked upright.

She pitched backward, but he managed to reach behind and grab her.

"Sorry," he said, then tapped the plans. "Look at this." He scanned the room. "There's a secret passage in the wall. It's not uncommon for the era, so I thought there might be, plus the walls are so thick, you can camouflage it. The opening's in this room, behind the bookcase."

He strode that direction and knocked on the wall, which

did sound hollow. "I wonder where the latch is. Did you know about it?"

"Not a clue." She joined him in the search. Had Randall known? Was it a secret passed from father to son? He'd been an only child, and he had no children. Why hadn't he told her about it? If the plans were in his desk, surely he'd known.

Had he used the passage?

"Where does it lead?" she asked.

"Looks like it runs between this room and the library then goes downstairs. Maybe into the wine cellar you showed me this morning. There might be an exit to the outside from there. Or there might not." He tried twisting carved wood curlicues and swirls in sequence down the wall.

"Do you think it was an escape route?" Dana asked.

"Built in 1908? Who knows? Usually secret passage-ways are found off bedrooms. A way to sneak the mistress in and out." He moved up a level, finally turning a silver wall sconce. The wall popped open a couple of inches. "A silver latch," he said, turning to her and grinning. He opened the door fully and peered in. "Undoubtedly an inside joke in the Sterling family. I saw a flashlight in the bottom desk drawer."

Dana found the flashlight and passed it to him, then followed him inside.

As secret passageways went, it was nothing special, just dark. She didn't have to squeeze to get through, but Sam had to angle his body a little. He kept the flashlight moving, not really lighting the path, but everything else. The air was stagnant, dry and dusty. She trailed her hand down the walls to steady herself, finding rough plaster and lathe.

She sneezed.

"Plenty of cobwebs," he said, spotlighting the ceiling, brushing at the wispy streams. "The dust on the floor has been disturbed, but I can't tell how recently."

Her finger snagged on something sharp. She snatched her

hand back then twitched her nose, trying to stop another sneeze. "I can't see where I'm going."

He reached for her hand.

Oh. Well. This is nice, she thought. He could keep her in the dark awhile longer.

She sneezed again.

"Arianna, I believe there are rats in the walls." Nate's voice, layered with humor, filled the passageway.

"With allergies," Arianna added.

"Look up there. It's a speaker," Sam said to Dana, spotlighting it, then another on the office-wall side. "Not exactly an early 1900s innovation." He shined the beam over the rest of the wall.

"Nate," he called out. "We're in a passageway between the rooms. If Dana's housekeeper gets back while we're still here, give us a shout."

"You got it."

"Let's keep going," he said, taking her hand again.

They inched along until they came to the end, then couldn't find a latch to open an exit door to the stairway. "Batteries are dying," he said, shaking the flashlight, the power fading. "I'll check it out again later. Let's head back to the office."

There was no way they could change places, so Dana led, although much more slowly, feeling her way. The light died. The batteries were probably years old. At the same moment they heard Nate greet Hilda and introduce himself and Arianna by name without explaining who they were.

Putting his hand on her back, Sam stopped Dana from going any farther.

"Where is Senator Sterling?" they heard Hilda ask.

"She went for a walk," Arianna answered. "We expect her back anytime now."

Dana's nose twitched again. Panicked, she pinched her nose and turned to him. "I'm going to sneeze," she whispered frantically.

"No, you're not."

His command struck her as funny. She tried to hold her nose and cover her mouth at the same time. "Oh, yes...I am. What are you...going to...do about it?"

He pulled her to him and wrapped her in both arms, pressing her face to his chest, muffling her, startling the sneeze right out of her but replacing it with something altogether different—need. Her nose touched the vee of skin where he'd removed his tie and undone his top two buttons.

"Will you be staying for dinner?" Hilda asked.

"We're not sure," Nate said. "We'll know more when the senator returns."

Dana heard Sam's heart beat, strong and steady. Wouldn't it be lovely to fall asleep to that soothing sound? She pressed her lips to the spot over his heart. He went perfectly still but his heart rate picked up.

"I've never known her to go for a walk and leave company behind," Hilda said, an edge to her voice.

"She said she needed air."

And Sam. I need Sam. She curved her arms up his back and felt him jerk. His mouth touched her hair, smothering a harsh breath, but there wasn't much he could do to stop her without making noise. He cupped her face and tipped her head back. They were poised to kiss but he didn't lower his mouth to hers. She felt his breath dust her face and knew what an effort he was making to resist her.

His resistance only encouraged her. She slipped her arms around his waist and pulled herself closer to him, feeling his response. She moved against him.

"Sam—"

He put his hand over her mouth then slid both hands over her rear, cupping her, lifting her into him, the effort to remain undetected both dangerous and exciting.

"We're not company," Arianna said in the next room, her tone all business. "We're working on a project for her."

Dana swallowed a groan and leaned back as Sam moved his mouth down her neck and into her cleavage. He nudged aside her blouse with his nose, dipped his tongue under the lacy edge of her bra. Her head touched the wall. She arched higher toward him. It was impossible to keep contact above and below the waist at the same time, yet she wanted both.

"I'll bring refreshments while you wait for the Senator," Hilda said.

Arianna said something about the offer being wonderful...or something. Dana didn't care. The darkness swallowed her. There was only touch, and no way of knowing where the next touch would come. He set his hands on her waist. She was afraid he would push her away, but he pulled her blouse free from her slacks, slowly, seductively, the drag of fabric against her skin almost painful. He unbuttoned her blouse and snapped open the front closure of her bra without fumbling. She'd have to think about that later.

He let her stand there without touching her, her breath uneven, her pulse racing. Then his hands covered her breasts with heat, startling her for a moment. His fingers sought her aching nipples, then at last his mouth. Ah, his mouth. Warm, wet, wonderful.

"What would you like?" Hilda asked.

Sam inside me. Right here. Right now. Dana arched higher as he drew on her nipples, squeezing the flesh around them. He slid a hand down her body, following her zipper, then lower.

"Some iced tea would be great," Nate said, his tone dismissive—or was it desperate?

Sam dragged his thumb along the seam of her jeans, stopping when she gasped, making a circular motion in the same rhythm he used with his mouth on her breast, twisting his body to accommodate the confines of the small space.

"Nothing to eat?" Hilda asked.

"No, thanks."

"Very well."

Oh. Very well, indeed. There, she thought, raising her hips. Don't stop. Don't stop. Don't—

"You'd better get out of there while you can, buddy," Nate said a moment later. "She's suspicious. She's probably going to look for Dana."

Noooo. She was right on the edge. Just one more touch, one more swirl of his tongue on her breast. A little more pressure down low—

She needn't have worried. He kept going until release slammed into her. She bit her lip as she came hard against his hand. She'd forgotten the power, the rush, the heat of sex. The oblivion.

Warm air bathed her damp body when he moved away from her. He was breathing as deeply as she.

She wanted to kiss him, not only to end the moment but to let him know what it meant to her. She reached out in the dark. Her hand bumped his chest.

"Get dressed," he ordered in a hard whisper.

She dragged her hand down him, wishing she could see him and glad she couldn't.

"Dana." The pleading tone could have meant for her to continue or to stop.

Testing, she molded her hand over him. He moved, one quick, hard lurch, as if trying to control an uncontrollable action.

He swore. His response filled her with power.

"No more." He encircled her wrist, stopping her. "No...more." He seemed to struggle to breathe. "Get...dressed."

The shifting of fabric filled the space around them. He put his hands on her hips and moved her forward. They stopped where they'd entered, listened for a few seconds, opened the door a crack.

Empty. They rushed into the room and latched the door, then straightened the items that had shifted on the bookshelves. She felt his gaze on her as she tucked in her blouse and ran her fingers through her hair. His silence said more than words.

"Don't you dare say that was a mistake," she said, lifting her chin. "Don't you dare."

"I—"

The office door opened. Hilda stood there. "You're home." She looked confused for a moment then slipped back into her designated role.

"Did you want something?" Dana asked, irritated, wishing she knew how Sam felt. He would undoubtedly take advantage of the interruption to change the subject.

"The people working in the library said you'd gone for a walk."

"I did."

"I didn't hear you come in. You weren't here when I got home." She seemed to really look at Dana then. Her eyes shifted to the bookshelves. She drew up a little taller. "I offered refreshments to your people."

"Thank you. They'll be staying for dinner, as well. Give us until seven o'clock, please."

"Yes, ma'am."

Hilda closed the door behind her.

"She knows about the passage," Sam said.

"Why do you say that?"

He pulled something from her hair. "She put one and one together. Cobwebs and you missing then reappearing without her hearing you."

"Do you think she uses it?"

"Not recently. In the past? I don't know. The speaker is more current technology, but either Randall or his father could've installed it."

"I can't figure out why he didn't tell me about the passage. I thought we shared everything." She sighed. "That's ridiculous, of course. I didn't tell him everything either, not the secrets I'd buried before I met him. Certainly not about how Harley tried to rape me."

She stopped short. Finally she'd said the humiliating words aloud. Sam's expression darkened. She couldn't understand how he could be willing to help her now after what she'd put him through fifteen years ago.

"I'm so sorry, Sam, for going to the police. I should've listened to you. You were right when you said Harley's father would stop an investigation cold. I thought you were being heroic. I didn't know naming you as a witness would put you in danger."

"What did happen to Harley? Anything?"

"After you left town, it came down to my word against his. The police chief told my parents that Harley had been given a 'good talking to,' so that he understood when a girl says no, it means no."

"Why were you with him? You never liked him."

"I had stayed after school for a student council party to celebrate graduation. Afterward he offered a bunch of us rides home." She took a deep breath, visualizing what she'd tried to put out of her head. "He left me for last. I tried to get out of the truck, but he grabbed my arm and held me. Then he dragged me into the woods." She closed her eyes. "He liked it when I fought him. He kept saying how he knew I wanted him and to stop acting like I didn't. God. My parents gave me a car the next day for graduation. The next day! I wouldn't have had to accept a ride with him—"

She stopped. This wasn't about her. It was about what Sam had done for her. "If I hadn't gone to the police, nothing would have happened to you."

"I survived. Let's move on. We've got a more important issue to face, like who wants you out of the political picture."

She admired his ability to stay focused. She enjoyed his quick, logical mind, the power he showed in subtle ways, even his occasional protectiveness. She'd made a mistake in not asking him from the beginning for his help, because he wasn't a man easily thwarted or daunted. Not to mention how appealing he was as a man, his strength and his tenderness.

She took a cue from him and refocused. "What's next, then?"

"Abe is talking to a few people, checking out some—"

"That's how you and my chief of staff keep something confidential, by bringing in more people?"

"Why are you so determined to try to solve this yourself? We can't do it without help from people who can work some aspects of the investigation much more efficiently than we can. After all these years you must know he'll be discreet. He knows the players. He'll make a few friendly calls. I think we need to focus on Harley. The timing is too right to ignore."

"I'd hoped never to see Harley again." She pressed a hand to her mouth. "Harley. He phoned in to Lilith's program—what day was it? Tuesday. She sent me a tape. It's in my briefcase." She called herself all kinds of names. "How could I forget something like that? I'll go get it."

"I'll be in the library checking on Nate and Arianna."

"Okay." She ran up the staircase, found the tape and a small tape player, then started toward the door. On the wall of her bedroom hung a picture from her wedding. She didn't look like a first-time bride. No flowing gown, no veil. Her simple pearl-pink suit seemed appropriate for a judge's-chambers wedding. Randall had seen no reason to wait. She'd agreed.

But she'd regretted not having the fairy tale. Oh, maybe not a five-hundred-guest extravaganza, but a gown that would make her feel like a princess walking down the aisle to her Prince Charming, and all her friends and family watching instead of just her parents and Lilith.

It had been so dignified, instead. *She* had become dignified.

She'd believed what she'd told Sam, that there was more to marriage than passion, but she'd been thinking only about sexual passion. There were other kinds of passions that mattered, too. But if anything, she'd become more emotionally controlled and composed.

She hadn't lost that passion completely. Being near Sam made that clear to her.

Well, if she needed things to change, it was up to her to change them. There was still time.

And there was a man downstairs who'd been her knight in shining armor three times now, without asking anything in return. A man who'd rekindled a fire inside her that he'd first lit in high school then rejected in a way she'd never understood.

Maybe he was afraid, too. She wanted him to give her a chance and see what could happen. The old flames could be used to torch new ones.

She could start tonight. She would change into something more feminine, freshen her makeup, spritz on a little perfume. She would smile at him, flirt with him.

If he would let her.

She tamped down her insecurities. He was good at picking up her signals and understanding them. Surely he would realize that she wanted to continue what they'd started in the passageway.

Sam watched Dana hunt down an electrical outlet for the portable tape player. She'd changed into a lacy, stretchy top and hip-hugging pants, taking five years off her normally conservative appearance, and removing all hints of her political status from view. He'd touched that skin underneath, tasted it, stroked it. He'd heard her sighs, felt her hands on him…

He caught Arianna watching him. No one was better at reading unspoken cues than she, the reason he almost always called her in on interviews. Sam was good at it, but Arianna was masterful.

Arianna and Nate also knew about his past with Dana, thanks to a night a few years ago when they thought they were going to die. In the dark hours while trapped and waiting to be rescued after a bombing of their army headquarters, they each shared their greatest success and deepest regret. Dana was the key player in his.

He was irritated now that Arianna knew. She wasn't one for letting such things slide. It didn't help that his sexual frustration with Dana had reached meltdown, then his mood blackened further when he heard Harley's voice on tape.

"I'm looking to help a woman lose her frigidity," Harley said.

Arianna laughed. Sam didn't think it was the least bit funny.

"Her frigidity," Lilith repeated slowly. "What exactly do you mean by that?"

"You know, she's cold. Maybe she's a hopeless cause, I don't know. I mean, if I can't help her, no man can."

"Tell me a little more about her."

"I have a name for her. The princess of Prospector High."

Two beats of silence passed. "I see. Since your title isn't exactly complimentary, why are you interested in her?"

"Because it just kills me that she's going through life without enjoyin' it."

"And you would be the one to bring her pleasure?"

"You bet I would."

"Maybe she just doesn't like you."

It was his turn to pause. "Well, now, that's not a professional thing to say to a man who's tryin' to help someone out, is it, *Dr.* Lilith?"

"I would say, caller, that the problem lies in your ego, not this woman's frozen desires. It sounds like a lost cause to me. My advice is to back away."

"Can't do that. It's my destiny. I won't be satisfied until I've taken care of this gal, that's for sure. Taken care of her but good."

"Frankly, I don't know how to break down this woman's defenses, caller. Better just move on to someone more receptive…I see it's time for a commercial."

"Lose her frigidity?" Arianna repeated, chuckling. "Pompous ass."

Dana's eyes finally took on some sparkle. "I see you've met him."

"Yeah, him and a few thousand others like him."

Nate chimed in. "And they all hightailed it outta there clutching their wounded crotches."

"That was for the part of *no* that they didn't understand."

"You ever said yes, Ar?"

She tossed a pen at Nate, who caught it midflight.

"Children," Sam said, pushing past the bubbling fury that wasn't going away. "I think it's time I paid a call on our old friend. Looks like I'll be going to the funeral with you, after all, Dana."

"You are not going to cause a scene at the funeral."

He hoped his expression said, What do you think I am, an idiot?

She held up her hands in surrender. "Just checking. You left me to deal with the aftermath of the scene you made at the reunion."

Arianna's eyebrows went up. "Sam made a scene? Surely you jest."

Dana warmed to the subject. Her eyes sparkled. "I'm not kidding. He swooped in, danced with me, caused a ruckus with Harley—after which Harley ended up on the floor, but no one could figure out how—then he swooped out. He was only missing the black cape. I caught hell for his superhero tactics."

"What do you mean? What did Harley do?" Sam asked, ignoring the teasing glint in her eyes. This was serious. Why hadn't he thought about the potential retribution in front of everyone at the dance? He'd guarded her house for hours in case Harley followed her home. But, dammit, he hadn't even thought about what could have happened at the reunion itself. What the hell was the matter with him?

"He was his usual arrogant self," Dana said. "I dealt

with it. But I was not too happy with you.'' She grinned, contradicting her words, then she walked to the door. ''I'm going to phone Candi and tell her I'll be attending the funeral. She wanted me to say a few words. And Lilith will want to know, too, although her husband says she's not going any distance in a car right now. I'll be back in a few minutes.''

The library door had no sooner closed behind her when Arianna leaned her elbows on the tables, rested her chin in her hands and raised her eyebrows again.

''What?'' Sam said.

''You.''

''What about me?'' But he knew. He knew.

''You are still gaga over the Honorable Dana.''

''So?''

''So, you've not only got to go to the funeral, you've got to act like her lover.''

''Why the hell would I do that?''

''See? You're not even thinking straight or you would know you don't have a choice. It'll tick off this Harley royally, then you'll see what he's got going, if anything. Something tells me it's a role you won't mind playing. In fact, you'd probably even like to play it again, Sam.''

Nate laughed.

Sam started to debate the point then realized Arianna was right. He had to make it look personal. And the more loverlike the better, if they intended to get a rise out of Harley. Sam was torn between agony and ecstasy—finally the right to touch her, but it was only a game. A role. A job.

''You realize you could be photographed there,'' Arianna said.

''It's a small-town funeral for a local teacher,'' he said, but more to convince himself.

''With a newsworthy woman attending and speaking.''

''Her decision is last minute. I don't imagine any press will attend.''

''But if they do?'' Nate asked. ''You know what you're

forfeiting? The speculation will start. Plus, if you drop out of the picture too soon after, it'll be further cause for curiosity.''

"I know. Odds are good it won't go beyond Miner's Camp.''

"A wishful statement from Dana's friend about her running for office again made it beyond Miner's Camp,'' Arianna pointed out.

"I know.'' He glanced at each of them, gauging their reaction. "If I'm identified, along with the firm, will you be okay with that?''

"Yes,'' Arianna said, then looked to Nate, who nodded. "But will you?''

"I don't want to cause a problem,'' Sam said. "We've never needed publicity to get work. Never sought it. One of the appeals of our firm is that we're a well-kept secret. That matters to the people who refer us and who hire us.''

"Bless their generous wallets,'' Nate said.

"If she knew what a risk you were taking, what a sacrifice you were making for her, would she let you?'' Arianna asked.

"I'm not telling her, and neither will you. This is my decision. My choice. It's better if she doesn't know so she doesn't have to lie. She's a really bad liar.''

"And she's a politician?'' Nate asked. "Look, the way I see it, unless you become a permanent item with Dana, it's not going to matter.''

Nate was right. Sam would do Dana this favor then walk away. The less she knew, the more protected she was from the wrong kind of attention. Her reputation was everything.

Hours later, Sam was still telling himself that as he turned out the library lights. Dana had invited them all to stay overnight. There were plenty of guest rooms. Sam made a quick trip to his hotel to pick up his clothes for the funeral the next day, then they'd shared a rich fish chowder that Hilda prepared. After, they burrowed into the library, again poring over files Abe had brought, including the threats and hate mail accumulated during the years.

At one point Arianna held up two letters. "Apparently, Senator, you're a liberal pig and a conservative prig."

Dana had looked amused. "Really? Let me see." She read the contradictory notes and smiled. "They're talking about the same piece of legislation, too."

"Do you respond to these letters?" Arianna asked.

"I thank them for expressing their views."

"Ah. How polite of you," Nate said.

"I'm known for my good manners."

Although they'd kept reading, Sam wasn't sure the answers were to be found in the past. The source of the threat appeared to be either Harley or someone with a political agenda.

He climbed the stairs, exhausted. He'd sent Dana to bed an hour ago when she fell asleep sitting up. Nate and Arianna lasted a half hour longer. Sam had stayed in the library just thinking until his eyes closed as well.

He walked down the hall toward his assigned guest room, came to her bedroom door and stopped. It was open a crack. He was tempted. Instead, he grabbed the handle to pull the door shut.

"Sam?"

She'd been waiting for him? He opened the door slightly but didn't look in. "What?"

The bedding rustled then she was pulling the door open, light from the hall bathing her. He didn't know what he'd expected her to wear but it wasn't the flannel pajama bottoms and a tank top that fit her like a second skin. Her hair fell over her shoulders to rest temptingly on the upper curve of her breasts. He clenched his fists.

"Do you want to come in?" she asked.

"No."

"You don't want to finish what we started this afternoon?"

He tried to read her expression. Her eyes didn't darken, her jaw didn't clench. "Good night, Dana."

"Wait. Are we attending the funeral together or separately?"

He crossed his arms. "We're going to have to pretend to have a relationship."

"We are?"

"Yeah. Nate and Arianna figure it'll bring out the truth from Harley if he's jealous."

"So, that means what? We hold hands or something?"

"Whatever the situation warrants."

The glint in her eyes might have pleased him another time. Women didn't often tease him—which said a lot about him, he supposed. He liked that Dana did.

"We might have to kiss?" she asked, moving in on him.

He didn't step back but he wanted to. A big step. A leap. A bound. "You might have to look at me like, you know."

"Like I'd like to have my way with you? Would you have to look at me like that, too?" she asked, enjoying this way too much.

"If it becomes necessary."

She laughed quietly. "You're so serious."

"That's what you're paying me for."

That stopped her momentarily, as he'd intended. Then she moved even closer.

"Your single-mindedness is a comfort, I admit, but if you could lighten up just a little, as Arianna and Nate sometimes do, I wouldn't feel so increasingly impotent."

"Don't hold your breath." He softened the words with a teasing tone.

She smiled. "You think we need to practice the kissing part," she said, "so it looks like we've done it a lot? We sort of skipped that this afternoon in the passageway, and last night's kiss in the garden was pretty tame."

Was she flirting? Dangerous move, if she was. What he felt for her wasn't the crush he'd had in high school but a

man's attraction to a woman. "I think I've got the skill to pull it off," he said coolly.

"I'm not sure I do."

"You were fine last night." It seemed like a month ago. "Good night."

He took a couple of steps.

"Sam?"

He heard an urgency in her voice and turned around.

"You said you keep a low profile. Won't this ruin that? Are you worried about—"

He hauled her into his arms, backed her into the room and against a wall, and kissed her. Devoured her. Absorbed her. She tasted like heaven. She made glorious little sounds of pleasure. She moved her body against his until they were molded together, heat to heat. Her fingers dug into his back, dragged lower then stopped on his rear. He did the same to her.

She whispered his name between kisses once, twice, then a third time with a new kind of demand. He gathered his resistance from an idiotic place inside his mind willing to give it up.

"Consider us practiced," he said then walked away as fast as his aroused body would let him. Sleep on that, Senator Sterling, he thought. You sleep on that.

Because he sure as hell wasn't going to.

Eight

They drew attention the moment they climbed out of Sam's car in the church parking lot. From behind his sunglasses Sam inspected his surroundings, his emotions a complicated mix of sorrow and pleasure. Only in his wildest fantasies had he imagined being in public with Dana on his arm. That they were there because his friend had died made the moment bittersweet. Mr. G. had always included news of Dana when he passed along information through the years, and his being friends with her parents meant the news was current.

He glanced at Dana walking beside him, greeting people with a nod, ignoring their curious stares. He recognized only a few people. Harley wasn't among them.

He forced himself to enter the church, then he and Dana were escorted to a front pew on the center aisle. He made a point of leaning and whispering to her, forcing her to angle closer. The gesture would look intimate, especially when she adjusted his tie, which he'd twisted to one side a little as they sat down. Once they were settled, however, his mind was free to wander from the job at hand.

The coffin was closed, and he was grateful for that. A photograph sat atop it that so captured the spirit of the man, it seemed as if he were there. That was how he should be remembered.

Sam pressed a hand to his jacket pocket and felt the shape of the valedictorian medal nestling there. An ache settled in his chest then spread. His arms and legs were like anchors caught in river mud.

Dammit. He needed to tune out. The last funeral he'd attended was his mother's, right here in this church, when he was ten years old. He'd sat in the same pew, his father beside him, reeking of whiskey, ignoring him. He could remember slicking back his hair with water and polishing his shoes by himself for the first time, a task his mother had done with him; she'd applied the polish, he buffed. He hadn't known how to iron, so his shirt was wrinkled. He'd pulled at it and pulled at it, trying to stretch out the wrinkles, but nothing helped. In desperation he'd tried to iron his shirt but had scorched a huge brown mark into the fabric. He'd cried in frustration, burying his head under a pillow so his father wouldn't hear.

Although he'd seen the Gianninis at church before, he'd never spoken to them. They took him under their wing when his father left him behind after the service. The memories were vivid. Rosa and her lavender-powder smell; Mr. G. and his kind, consoling voice. They'd seemed old to him at the time, but they were only in their early fifties.

Sam reached for Dana's hand, pulling it into his lap, linking fingers. He felt her silent question but didn't—couldn't—answer. The minister came through a side door with Rosa, her arm tucked in his, her gray hair beauty-parlor perfect, as always. The minister seated her next to family members in the aisle seat opposite Sam's. When she saw him, breathtaking grief crumpled her face. She started to rise. Sam excused himself from Dana and went to her, kneeling down, accepting an embrace surprisingly strong from a woman not even five feet tall.

"You came," she said, her lavender scent making its way past the many floral tributes on display. "Thank you, Sam. It means so much."

"If you ever need anything, Rosa, I'm a phone call away. Promise you'll call."

"Sweet boy, of course."

He heard a low buzz of conversation as he returned to his seat.

"I hadn't realized you were close to the Gianninis," Dana whispered, brushing something from his jacket. "It makes sense now. He's the one who kept you informed."

He stared straight ahead. "He loved me. After my mother died he and Rosa were the only ones who loved me."

Sam couldn't believe he'd said those words. The scene in front of him blurred. He swallowed.

"Oh, Sam," she said quietly, tenderly. "I'm so sorry."

Suddenly he was glad he'd come, glad that it made Rosa happy. He was learning that confronting his past was the only way to make room for his future.

The service started. Hymns were sung, several people spoke, Dana being the last. Sam admired her poise and grace as she walked to the podium. She was accustomed to the spotlight, but her warmth won people over, not her notoriety.

"We called him Mr. G.," she began. "Not because his name was a tongue twister to pronounce, although it was, but because he was respected and loved in equal measure."

The short but eloquent speech described her early memories of him at backyard barbecues with her parents, of math puzzles he always maneuvered people into trying, of his heart and kindness and philanthropy. When she was through, she stopped to hug Rosa before returning to her seat.

Sam put his arm around her and brushed her hair with

his lips, more for his comfort than hers, inhaling her perfume. At some point today he'd stopped playing the role he'd intended but had slipped back into the one of years ago, his heart in danger again—and with nothing really changed. She was still unattainable.

After the burial everyone moved from the church cemetery into the hall for a buffet and conversation. Dana didn't want to spend hours talking with people. She wanted to let some things settle in, like Sam's surprising connection with the Gianninis. On the other hand she was so enjoying his attention that she wanted to linger in public.

His complexity tempted her in ways no other man had, and the pleasure of holding his hand was one she didn't want to give up.

She felt him draw her away from the crowd slightly. His voice was hushed. "I know it's important that you mingle, but I can't allow you to do it alone. I apologize up front for not letting you have any private conversations. At this point, everyone is suspect."

"It's okay. I understand. Harley just got here."

"Yeah, I saw him pull in to the parking lot."

"His timing is amazing. He skips the funeral but makes sure he arrives in time for the schmoozing."

"Or," Sam said, "he heard you were here."

"With you," she added.

"Isn't it interesting that we so easily threaten him."

Dana would have responded except that Rosa came up to them right then and accepted more hugs.

"I heard you're working with the high school to start a math scholarship in Ernie's name," Rosa said to Sam. "That the entries will come to me to choose a winner each year."

"Details to come. Is there anything I can do for you?" he asked.

Dana found it interesting that Sam changed the subject so quickly. Was he the driving force behind the scholarship or the monetary backing or both? And why wouldn't he want recognition?

"I'm doing all right for now," Rosa said. She turned to Dana. "I hadn't heard you were…a twosome."

"It's a recent development."

"Well, you should know a few things about this young man."

"Rosa," Sam cautioned.

"What? I didn't promise to keep secrets. Ernie did."

"When you're married, keeping a secret applies to both spouses."

"Is that so? And just when did you become an expert on the matter?"

"At this very moment."

"Because it's convenient for you. Either go away or keep your mouth shut. I have something to say to Dana." She turned her back on Sam. "I haven't met anyone who has come as far as Sam. He had every right to be bitter. Instead he raised himself and took his responsibilities much more seriously than that drunkard of a father deserved."

"Please," Sam said. "It was long ago."

Dana felt the extent of Sam's discomfort but was so fascinated with the topic, she wouldn't have dreamed of stopping Rosa from talking.

"You see? He can't take a compliment because they were never given to him. Yet even before he was a teenager he was doing odd jobs to help pay for rent and food."

"Odd jobs provided by the Gianninis," he interjected. "For more money than the jobs were worth."

The older woman ignored him. "He added more responsibility every year, covered more of the expenses. After he left, he sent money to Ernie every month to help take care of that man who didn't deserve to call himself a father. Sam paid for his funeral and a proper burial." She put a hand on his arm. "You didn't owe him that. You didn't owe him anything. I know I've embarrassed you, Sam, but someone other than me needs to know the truth about you.

You had a stigma attached to you because of your father. It wasn't fair.''

"Life isn't fair."

"Don't spout clichés at me, young man."

Rosa invited the minister to join them as he approached, then others came along. Harley hovered on the fringes, squinting at Dana and Sam and their joined hands.

"Even Harley wouldn't make a scene here," Sam said quietly. "We need to go outside. He'll follow."

He chose the side of the church that faced the parking lot instead of the cemetery, Dana noticed. They sat on a wooden bench and waited.

"Are you sure this is going to work?" she asked after a few minutes.

"It would be out of character for him to let an opportunity slip by. His ego took a big hit at the reunion."

A van pulled in to the parking lot, the logo of a Sacramento news station on the side. Out hopped a cameraman and woman reporter. Harley conveniently wandered outside at that moment.

"Gee, I wonder who's responsible for a TV crew showing up," Dana said, then realized what it could mean to Sam. "What now?"

"We see it through."

"Sam. I can't ask this of you. I can't. Just go away until the cameraman is gone. Please. I'm not going to be responsible for taking away your privacy."

"I knew it would be a possibility."

How much debt could she owe him? "Do I explain you?"

"It doesn't matter what you say. Harley will give them my name."

"Senator Sterling," the reporter called out. "May I have a few minutes of your time?"

The camera was rolling.

Dana and Sam stood. "I'm here in a personal capacity today. I won't be making a public statement."

"Yes. I understand this—" she referred to her notes "—Ernest Giannini was a teacher?"

"A wonderful teacher and an old family friend."

The reporter shoved the microphone at Sam. "Did you know the deceased?"

"Everyone who went to high school here knew him," Dana said as Sam stood mute. She liked that he was going to make it hard for them. "I'm not news here, however. You need to go inside and talk to his family and the rest of the people who loved him."

"Senator, have you made a decision about reelection?"

She kept her tone even. "A friend of mine passed away this week. This day is about him. That's all I have to say."

The reporter gave the cut signal to the cameraman. "Off the record, Senator?"

"His name was Ernest Giannini, and he was an amazing man," Dana responded with a smile. "Go talk to his wife, Rosa. She'll tell you."

"It'll be interesting to see if they use any footage," Sam said after they left. Harley stopped the reporter outside the hall. She wrote in her notebook. "You know the story they're after is about how one of the state's most eligible women is finally showing up in public with a date."

"I hope it hasn't ruined things for you."

"People will forget me."

She knew it was a throwaway line designed not to make her feel guilty, but it hurt. "You underestimate people's interest in my love life. After the official year of mourning passed, I could feel a lot of attention toward me about when I would date. Who I would date. And the most interesting part was how women related to me."

"In what way?"

"They talked to me about their husbands more. Complained more, actually. As if I should be *glad* I didn't have to deal with a husband's flaws and quirks anymore."

He tipped his head and smiled. "Who's underestimating now, Dana? If they were telling you the down and dirty about their husbands, it was because they perceived you as a threat and were warning you off.''

Dana hadn't considered that. Why would she be a threat? In her business she dealt with more men than women, but it was just that, business.

Harley swaggered over. ''Well, well, well. Aren't we cozy? The Princess and the Loser. Think Hollywood would be interested?''

''Jealous?'' Sam asked.

He hitched up his pants. ''You may think you're the chosen one, Little Miz Dana, but I've got news for you. You aren't as popular as you think. I wouldn't run again if I was you.''

Dana felt Sam tense. ''You trying to give me advice, Harley? You?'' she asked.

''Just tellin' it like it is. People gave you a lot of leeway before 'cause they felt sorry for you, but this time it'll be different.'' He leaned toward her. ''I know somethin' about you, Miz Clean as a Whistle.''

''Are you threatening me?''

''Me? Never. I'm just remindin' you, bitch—''

Sam slammed him against the wall then kneed him in the groin to keep him there. Harley's white Resistol tumbled from his head to the ground.

''Let him go,'' Dana said urgently. ''The cameraman…''

When Sam released him, Harley almost lost his footing. ''Did you get that?'' Harley called to the cameraman, who'd hefted his camera on his shoulder but was too late to film the confrontation. He and the reporter kept walking toward their van. Harley swiped his hat from the ground and dusted it off. ''Feelin' pretty safe with your bodyguard, huh, Dana?''

''As a matter of fact, yes.''

He jammed his hat on his head, tipped it down low over his forehead. ''You were a prissy thing even in high school.''

''And you were always an idiot.'' People began to mill

out of the building. Several slowed down to see what was going on as they walked toward their cars. She didn't need more rumors than were already in the mix. "Let's go tell Rosa goodbye, Sam."

The men challenged each other with heated stares before they went in separate directions. She and Sam tracked down Rosa and managed to speak a few minutes with her.

In the car, Sam headed north instead of south. "Where are you going?" Dana asked.

"On the drive here you said we needed to check your parents' house."

She'd forgotten. "That's good, I suppose. I think we both could use a little unwinding," she added.

"Driving unwinds me."

"Well, I need a break."

He didn't answer but took the turnoff when he reached it.

"Do you think he's the one?" she asked.

"Subtlety's not his strong suit. I don't know if he'd have enough patience for the postal service. His threat today was aimed directly at you. It doesn't follow with what's happened until now. Unless he's not alone in the game."

"Meaning he's joined with a political enemy?"

"Right, although doubtful. Either way, it's a threat."

"Why didn't you say anything to him?"

"You were handling him just fine, Dana, and doing a very good job of riling him. I needed to see him react to you, not me."

"I can't believe how fast you pinned him."

"He's gotten a little soft since his football days."

"So you honestly don't think he's behind the threat?"

"Not what you've been receiving through the mail. That's got to be someone who knows you would take a bullet for Randall's reputation over your own. Harley doesn't care about that." He spared her a quick glance. "Do you know what he was talking about when he called you clean as a whistle?"

She looked at the road instead of Sam. "Yes."

"Something you haven't told me?"

She nodded. "Honestly, I'd forgotten about it."

"Could it damage your reputation?"

They were pulling in to the driveway of her parents' house. "I don't know. I was seventeen. And the charges were dropped."

Nine

—

Sam's only visit inside Dana's house had come the night he picked her up for the senior prom. He'd thought she must be rich. They had art on the walls and furniture that all looked good together. He realized now how mistaken he'd been. The nice but completely middle-class home had only been special because Dana lived there.

He took off his jacket and tie as she opened a window to air out the stuffy living room.

"I'll make lemonade," she said.

He wanted to know what she'd done that could've gotten her arrested. "I don't need anything."

"I do."

Her tone was anything but pleasant. He assumed it wasn't personal but directed at Harley, and her situation, and life in general. He trailed her into the kitchen, watched her slam a can of frozen lemonade on the counter, followed by a plastic pitcher that bounced noisily, and tipped, landing on the floor.

She grabbed the edge of the counter and swore. This behavior was so out of character for her, he waited and watched her until she seemed to gather herself then he picked up the pitcher and moved her aside to rinse it.

"Sorry," she muttered.

"You've held up well, Dana. No need to apologize."

"I haven't slept much. It makes me cranky."

"Fire away. I can take it."

His words seemed to take the steam out of her.

"I could really use a hug," she said, not waiting for a response but burrowing into him, locking her arms tight, resting her head against his shoulder.

He gave himself up to the moment, as he seemed to be doing too often, and even wrapped her close. Still she didn't relax.

"I don't know what I'd do without you," she said, her voice tight.

"Wait'll you get my bill."

Her laugh was shaky. "Yeah. Thank God I'm stinkin' rich, 'cause money sure does buy happiness, doesn't it?" Her bitterness hung in the air.

"Tell me about a time you were happy." He combed her hair with his fingers as she settled more comfortably against him.

"Grad school. I rented this tiny cottage in Berkeley. Bedroom you could squeeze a twin bed and dresser into. Living room where a twelve-inch TV seemed like a big-screen, you were sitting so close to it. Kitchen where you couldn't plug in two appliances at once. I loved it. I loved being at Cal. The campus environment, the midnight discussion groups and the laid-back atmosphere. I worked in Randall's office and I got to meet incredible people and be on the inside of political debates and decisions. It was amazing." She sighed. "Your fingers are incredible. I could sleep right here."

"Why don't you? Sleep, I mean. I can work by phone for a while. You could snatch a couple hours."

"You don't mind? Really?"

"I don't mind."

"Okay."

She took a step back and his body temperature plummeted. She looked fragile, yet he knew she wasn't. She picked up the can of lemonade.

"What are you doing?" he asked.

"Making you something to drink before I go upstairs."

"I hate lemonade."

Her mouth tightened. "Well, why didn't you say so?" She returned the can to the freezer then shut the door not quite hard enough to be called a slam but close.

Her foul mood was obviously back. He decided not to remind her that the lemonade was her idea.

"Go back to your happy place, Dana."

After a second, she laughed. "You know what else made me really happy?"

"I can't imagine."

"It's upstairs. If you want to come with me, I'll show you."

Creaky stairs, faded wallpaper, a sturdy banister. A lived-in, loved-in house, Sam thought. There would be lots of happy memories for her here. He followed her into her bedroom. He knew which room it was because he'd made it a point to know. Sometimes he would be out hiking and end up on her property. Because it was dense with trees, no one ever discovered him.

Her room looked as if it hadn't been touched since she left for college. Had she brought Randall here? Slept with him in the bed covered with a hot-pink and lime-green bedspread and piled with a variety of stuffed frogs? Sam couldn't picture Randall in this room where movie-ticket stubs were still tucked into the mirror frame and photographs tacked onto corkboard on the wall. It was all so decidedly girlie, he couldn't match it to Dana.

She'd disappeared into a small walk-in closet filled with clothes and boxes. In a minute she came out carrying a bundle wrapped in a fabric printed with pink hearts. She set it on the bed and opened it, taking out a picture frame and passing it to him, her expression too serious to think this could be a happy memory.

It was the prom. Their prom. Him in his rented tuxedo, her in flowy pink, paler than her usual hot pink, more sedate. He could still feel the fabric against his fingers, not silk as she wore now, but an imitation of some kind.

"I was happy that night. Most of the night, anyway," she said. "What happened, Sam? What did I do? I thought everything was fine, then all of a sudden you changed. It had been a great date until then."

He couldn't answer without explaining her father's role in the evening. Aware she was waiting for his reaction, he took the photograph from her. "We were so young," he said.

"I think we look cute together. Please tell me what happened that night. I know it was just a sympathy date for you, but for me—"

"Sympathy? Where the hell did you get that idea?"

"What else could I call it? I had a date lined up. He broke his leg right before the prom. You said, 'I'll take you.' Everything was good, then you stopped dancing with me. You all but stopped talking, too. You didn't kiss me good-night."

"Dana, I guarantee you it was no sympathy date. It was a carpe diem date."

"Seize the day? Why?"

She really didn't know? She never knew how he felt about her? Three days before the prom he'd overheard her telling Lilith and Candi after English class that she couldn't go to the dance. There'd been tears in her eyes and crushing disappointment in her voice. The minute her friends took off for their next class he volunteered. No one could've pulled him down from the clouds after she said yes.

No one except her father.

"I always liked you," Sam said finally, feeling somewhat adolescent.

"Then why did it end so badly?"

"I'd never kissed a girl. I didn't want my inexperience to show."

"Are you serious?"

"Yeah. The more the night went on, the more nervous I got." Which was a partial truth anyway. He'd been dying to kiss her but was scared to mess it up.

"Something tells me there's more to it than that, but you obviously don't want to share." When she met his gaze she frowned. "That night...Sam, that night must have cost you a fortune. You worked so hard for what you had. I didn't know how hard until listening to Mrs. Giannini today."

He shrugged. It had cost him almost every penny of his savings, that's all. He'd spent the money without regret.

But he wanted this picture. How could he ask without seeming pathetic?

Just then she picked up a folder from within the heart-decorated fabric the photo was wrapped in. "Here's a copy for you, if you want it. I bought them as a surprise that night. I never gave it to you because... Well, because I thought you hated me."

"No."

She sighed. "Don't you wonder how we survive being teenagers? It's such a self-absorbed time. Everything is so important and serious. We make assumptions. We waste precious time being wrong because we won't ask for clarification. I should've asked you what was wrong that night. I wish I'd had enough faith in myself to ask you."

"You didn't do anything wrong. I wish the date had ended differently, too, but I guess things work out the way they're supposed to."

"Do you think we were supposed to meet again at the reunion?"

"I think fate plays a role sometimes." He watched her take the toy frogs off the bed and fold down the bedspread.

"If Mr. G. hadn't died, we wouldn't be here, alone." She undid two buttons on her suit jacket. Something frilly peeped out, black lace. "Do you know how seldom I'm alone? I feel alone a lot, but there are usually people around."

"I'm around."

"You know what I mean. Out of the public eye, even if that eye is only Hilda."

She stood still, as if waiting for him to leave. But all the memories that had surfaced since seeing her again started to pool in his mind, then transformed to desire, low in his body. His gaze strayed down her, head to toe. He didn't care that she was watching him look at her. He wanted her. Not as the boy he'd been but as the man he'd become. He wouldn't have known what to do with her then, but he knew now. Needed her now.

He took a step toward her, touched a button on her jacket, slipped it through the hole. She said nothing, just watched him with dark, serious eyes. He undid one more button, then the last. Still, she didn't move.

He slipped her jacket off and tossed it over a white-wicker rocking chair. The black lace bra was cut low and pushed her breasts into smooth mounds.

His hands found hers and he lifted them to his lips, then held them until he knew this was what she wanted, too, and the quaking subsided.

"I have protection," he said.

She looked startled for a moment, then she eased closer. "Do you? Had you anticipated this, then?"

"No." He just hadn't trusted that something wouldn't happen, not after yesterday in the passageway, and last night at her bedroom door. And this morning when he'd awakened from the most vivid sex dream he could remember having.

He reached behind her to unzip her skirt. It fell to the

carpet with barely a sound. She wore a thong and black thigh-high stockings. The sight of her almost staggered him. He'd dreamed of seeing her like this since a day in tenth grade when her nipples had gone hard, pressing against her blouse while he and Dana argued a point from history class about Napoleon.

He tamed the memory. "I'm never going to be able to watch you on C-SPAN again, Senator, knowing what you wear under those power suits."

She smiled in return, a teasing, sultry look that darkened her eyes impossibly.

Assured he wouldn't have to stop this time, he took charge, diving his fingers into her hair, tipping her head back and finding her mouth with a passion so long denied, so long fantasized that he backed off almost instantly, afraid he would hurt her.

"Don't think," she whispered as she had once before, moving against him, her body soft and yielding and inviting, her hands coming to rest at his waist. "Just do."

He didn't need any more encouragement. Maybe it was wrong. Maybe it was stupid. But she was what he needed. He wouldn't be left with regrets this time.

Ah, but she felt glorious. Her hair brushing against his arms, her hands running along his chest, finding buttons, pulling at fabric. Her mouth, hot and sweet and demanding. The tempting sounds that vibrated along her throat when he stopped to taste on his way down. Her fragrance, made more potent with body heat. The curve of her back as she offered her breasts. The click of her bra clasp. The velvety texture of her nipple as he circled it with his tongue, then pulled it into his mouth, making her cry out, encouraging him toward the other one. Do more. Go further. Take her higher. The smooth, long length of her body as he knelt to take off her shoes and stockings. The feel of her hands on his head when he pressed his mouth to the black thong. The exquisite pain of her fingers molding his skull, digging in, while he traced the edges of the fabric with his tongue.

The silky smoothness of her legs as he grazed her skin with his fingertips.

He pressed her onto the bed, yanked off the rest of his clothes, then peeled her thong away. He covered her body with his, wishing he had the will to take it more slowly, knowing he couldn't last long. He slipped a hand down her to test her response. She rose to meet his hand, moaned as he slid a finger into her, drew a quick hard breath when he swirled his thumb up higher.

She was ready; he was beyond ready.

He stopped long enough to protect them, long enough to look in her eyes and be sure this was okay and right and good for her. Her eyes shimmered, her cheeks flushed, her lips parted.

"Sam," she said. That was all. Just his name. Said like no one ever had. No one had wanted him like this, needed him like this.

He watched her face as he joined with her. Saw her un-mitigated pleasure, felt the urgency in her motions. She arched high, made a long, low sigh when he was sheathed. Her legs slid around him and locked. She dug her fingers into his rear, lifting herself higher still. Her release started slow and gained strength fast, the sounds pouring into the room, filling his head with sweet memories he could conjure up in years to come. When she started up a second time, he gathered her close and went with her, his pastel dream turning into Technicolor reality that dazzled and blinded and dazed. He'd felt nothing like it in his life. Nothing so perfect, so grand, so exquisite.

Except maybe the way she melted into him when they settled back on earth and whispered his name and fell asleep, trusting him to keep her safe, the highest compliment anyone could give him.

A wonderful ache spread through Dana as she awakened. She glanced at the clock. She'd slept for two hours, had fallen asleep in Sam's arms. She couldn't feel his weight beside her now, though, and turned her head to look for him.

He stood at the window, fully dressed, his hands in his pockets. She'd hoped they could shower together and make love once more before heading home, where life was bound to intrude.

Apparently life had already intruded.

She pulled the sheet to her chin as she rolled toward him, feeling even more naked with him dressed. "Hi."

He turned. After a slight hesitation he walked to the bed and sat facing her.

"Did you sleep at all?" she asked, examining his face for clues to his mood.

"No."

"Did you work?"

He shook his head.

"Postcoital conversation not your thing, huh?" she asked, trying to lighten the moment.

"A common complaint among women, I understand," he said.

She wanted to keep things breezy between them, then found she couldn't. "Are you regretting that we made love?"

He hesitated a few seconds. "Only as it affects the way we work together."

"How will it affect that?"

"It just will."

"I won't let it," she said, sure of it.

"You won't be able to help it," he answered with certainty.

"You seem to be speaking from experience."

"No." He framed her face with his hands and kissed her, a long, lingering kiss that made her eyes sting and her throat ache, then he rested his hands on her shoulders. "I just know how these things work."

She wrapped her hands around his wrists. The sheet drifted to her waist. "Is it because you did all the giving and I only took? You didn't give me any opportunity to return any favors, you know, especially yesterday. I'd hoped to make up for that.''

"Dana.'' He covered her breasts with his hands. "You are a strong, sexy woman. I didn't feel the least bit slighted. It just…complicates things.''

"Meaning, you're going to keep your distance? This amazing, incredible, satisfying experience won't be repeated?''

From outdoors the crunch of gravel under tires drew their attention. Someone was pulling in to the driveway.

Sam went to the window as Dana scrambled out of bed and began hunting down her clothes. "Silver Taurus,'' he said.

"I don't know who that could belong to.'' She put on her thong inside out and didn't care. Her bra was twisted into knots.

"Toss it to me,'' he said.

She did, then grabbed her stockings. By the time she'd put them on, he'd untangled her bra.

"Who is it?'' she asked, breathless, as she shimmied her skirt over her hips and grabbed her jacket.

"Haven't gotten out of the car. They're probably debating who's parked in the driveway in front of— Okay, doors are opening.'' He paused. "Well, Senator, unless I miss my guess, I'd say it's your parents.''

Ten

An hour after sunset, Dana kissed her parents goodbye then climbed into Sam's car. She glanced at his profile as they backed out of the driveway. What a difference a day makes, she thought as they headed back to the city. Last night she'd ached to make love with him. Now she had. And now she saw him in a different light, one more intense, more curious. There were so many questions to ask.

Her mom and dad's spur-of-the-moment decision to fly from Florida for the funeral had interrupted the intimacy building between her and Sam, although Dana blessed the rain gods for the Dallas thunderstorms that had delayed her parents for hours. They'd arrived at the church just after Dana and Sam left, staying on with Rosa for several hours after, and planned to return to Florida to drive their motor home back. If not for the thunderstorm, however, Dana wouldn't have been alone with Sam.

If her parents were surprised to see him, they didn't show it. Perhaps Rosa had alerted them? Sam had gone downstairs in time to greet them at the door while Dana brushed her hair and fixed her makeup, and summoned some degree of calm.

Again she looked at Sam, illuminated by the dashboard lights. He'd spoken little during dinner. Same for her father. Maybe it would've been hard to get any words in, anyway, given how much her mother talked, but still...

Sam had been too quiet. Then he'd become more so after her father offered to take him on a tour of the property after dinner. They'd been gone fifteen minutes, and Sam's expression was even more somber on his return. She'd wanted to hug him and say everything would be all right, but she had no idea why he seemed vulnerable.

Her heart ached but she didn't know why—

Yes, she did, she realized. She was falling in love with him, the thought spinning through her, gathering speed and heat.

"Why were you arrested?" he asked now, startling her.

She brushed at her skirt, striving for a casual look. "For possession of marijuana."

"What?"

His shock made her smile. "For possession—"

"I heard you. I just don't believe you. It's impossible."

"Thank you for the vote of confidence. Where were you when I got hauled in?"

"I don't know. Where was I? Why didn't I know about it?"

"Because it was after graduation and you were long gone."

"What happened?"

She let herself go back to that time and place. A night much like tonight. Summer. Warm. Only a few carefree weeks left before heading to college. She'd taken a job as a library aide during the day but the nights were hers. She and her friends were going to enjoy their last summer together before they headed in different directions, Willow to San Diego State, and Lilith and Dana to Cal. No college for Candi. She was getting married. The wedding was a week away.

"The girls and I had taken Candi out on the town for her bachelorette party. We'd been to Sacramento, but since we weren't old enough to drink, we didn't find a lot to do. We came home early enough to stop in at a party that Marsha Crandall was throwing. Remember Marsha?"

"Original party girl."

Dana nodded. "Her parents were out of town. I don't know what possessed me to go. Lilith talked me into it, I think, but Candi and Willow wanted to go, too. I figured Harley might be there and I wanted to avoid a confrontation with him."

"Was he there?"

"Yes. Aside from sending menacing glances my way, he left me alone, though. I figured his talk with the police chief had straightened him out. Anyway, there were a couple of kegs of beer, but I didn't drink because I was driving."

"The others did?"

"Yeah."

"Let me guess. You got stopped on the way home by the police—even though you weren't speeding and hadn't broken any law. The officer stuck his head in the car, smelled beer, hauled you all out, made a search for open containers, but instead found some pot that Harley had planted in your car."

"I assumed that, too, but Lilith started acting weird. I mean, all three of them were scared, because they'd been drinking and were underage, but Lilith was frantic. When the cop held up the plastic bag, she squeezed my hand so hard I thought she'd broken some bones."

"It was hers?"

"Yes."

"You didn't know she smoked pot?"

"I knew. I didn't know she carried it with her."

"It's hard to believe. You listen to her talk show and she has zero tolerance for drugs."

"People learn from their mistakes."

He glanced at her. "You took the fall for her."

She nodded.

"She let you?" He swore. "That's how your best friend—"

"Stop. There's more to it than that, Sam. You remember I skipped a grade? I'd turned seventeen in January. In fact, Lilith was the only one who was eighteen. So even though the driver of the car is legally responsible, because Lilith was the only adult, she would've been."

"So? It was her pot."

"Yes, it was, but it would've ruined her life. She'd gone beyond marijuana, had been experimenting with other things. It frightened me so much, but nothing I said stopped her. I also knew her, and I was sure this would scare her straight and turn her around. I was right, too. Not only did she never get into trouble after that, she's done great things."

"How did you get her out of it?"

"I said I'd taken the pot away from someone at the party for their own good. The police didn't believe me, of course, and I refused to give them names. As far as they were concerned I was a typical teenager trying to dodge the blame. I got hauled into the station, took some drug and alcohol tests, which were negative, but they still made me go to rehab classes. It helps to have your father on the council that appoints the police chief. The chief handled the situation quietly. You know…I'd never gotten in trouble before. I was headed for college. And so on and so on. They just dealt with it privately."

"Harley's father was on the council, too."

"Which is why Harley got off with barely a slap on the wrist for attacking me. Anyway, they never officially charged me with anything—that was the deal we made which sent me to the classes. Even if I had been charged and convicted, the records would've been expunged after seven years.''

''How did Harley know about your arrest?''

''His father's ties with the police chief, I suppose. Who knows. His reference to it today was the first he's made. But our paths hadn't crossed again until the reunion.''

''The only way this information could hurt you is by planting doubts about your character in the voters' minds.''

''Sometimes that's all it takes.''

''It's not clicking for me. Marijuana's not seen as such a big deal anymore. The same stigma isn't attached, for all that it's still illegal.'' He gave her a quick look. ''What did your parents do?''

''They were furious, of course, and disappointed in me. I stuck with the story I told the police, though, and I only got a lecture on thinking things through, on anticipating the consequences. Added to what had happened to you because of my 'good intentions,' it was more than enough to turn me into a model citizen.''

''You can hardly call yourself a delinquent because you reported Harley's rape attempt and the fact you covered for a friend, Dana.''

''I know. But I grew up fast that summer. My mom never sees the dark side of anything, and she kept looking at me as if I were a stranger. She would pat my back and offer sage advice until I almost couldn't keep a straight face.'' Dana wondered whether this would be the best time to ask about his mother, here in the car where he didn't have to make eye contact and the outside world barely intruded. ''Was your mom like that?''

His silence was deafening, making her aware of the road again, the sharp curves and dark path ahead of them. She watched his hands as he steered into the next bend. His speed didn't pick up, but his knuckles turned white.

Damn. She squeezed her eyes shut, berating herself. What a stupid thing to say to him! His mother had died because of injuries from a car accident on this road.

"My mother gave me a lot of advice, yes," he said at last.

Okay. Her fists unclenched. He would have changed the subject if he didn't want to talk about her. "Like what?"

"Life lessons. You know, how to behave in certain situations. What she expected of me."

"Do you remember specific advice?"

He hesitated. "Only the day before she died, in the hospital. No one told me she wasn't expected to live, but I knew. She wouldn't let herself rest. She would close her eyes for a few minutes, worn out, then blurt out something else. Every word took a little more out of her, but even at ten I recognized her need to talk."

Dana wished he would elaborate.

"He blamed me for her death," he said, sudden and harsh.

"Your father?"

He nodded once.

A cold fist of horror twisted her stomach. "But I thought— Wasn't he the one driving?"

"Yeah." The word came out like sandpaper. "We were going to the movies for my birthday. We'd never been as a family before—it was rare that we did something fun together. I was happy. He kept yelling at me to shut up. I could see his eyes in the rearview mirror, and they were mean, like always, but nothing could get me down. He told my mother to shut me up. She tried to explain that I was just happy. He backhanded her.

"I saw her head hit the passenger window. I heard how hard she connected."

The change in his voice scared Dana. He wasn't with her anymore. He'd returned to the horrifying moment. She wrapped a hand around his arm. "Sam."

Nothing.

"Sam, there's a pullout right after this turn. I want you to pull over there."

"I'm okay."

"I'm not. Pull over."

He did. "You weren't in danger," he said as he slowed to a stop then shoved the car into Park.

"Tell me the rest of what happened."

Holding on to the steering wheel, he stared out the windshield. A long pause ensued, then, "I unfastened my seat belt to try to help her. I leaned over the seat. He knocked me alongside the head and lost control of the car at the same time. We spun off the road. A tree stopped us, caving in Mom's side of the car. She had so many injuries. Multiple broken bones, lacerated organs."

Poor little boy. Such a heavy burden to carry for all his life. "Had he been drinking?"

"Not enough for a DUI, but he'd had a couple of beers. He always did. And he was always angry. He just got worse when he was drunk. I usually hid."

"Did you believe him when he blamed you?"

He nodded.

"Oh, Sam."

"He reinforced it every day... Every single day."

Dana wanted to comfort him, but he wouldn't look at her. She knew he wouldn't want to be seen as vulnerable. That made her hurt more for him, that need to prevent his emotions from surfacing. Be a man. She wondered how many times his father had said that to him.

"It wasn't my fault," Sam said, low and hoarse, as if he'd finally convinced himself.

"No. It wasn't your fault."

The dome light came on suddenly as he opened the door and climbed out. Although the headlights were on, he didn't walk to the front of the car. She decided to follow.

He hadn't gone far, only about twenty feet. He was standing with his arms crossed, his head down, his body swaying. She didn't try to sneak up on him. Her shoes crunched rocks and twigs. She stopped in front of him.

"I hated that son of a bitch. I dreamed about killing

him," he said. "Night after night. But I never hit him back, even when I got big enough to. He wasn't worth it."

"You were so smart to see that, to understand what it would've done to your life."

"Another deathbed lesson from Mom. And a promise, too." He lifted his head then, letting her see into his heart. "I loved her."

Dana's eyes filled with tears that slipped down her cheeks in scalding-hot rivers against the night air. "And she loved you, with all her heart."

He seemed to retreat a little. "Don't cry for me, Dana."

She cried harder, wishing she could take away some of the pain and guilt he'd carried with him for so long. He touched her then. First her hair, his hands moving over her lightly, shaking, stroking. "Shh, shh," he said. "It's all right. It's all right."

"It's not all right," she fired back, the words scraping along her throat. "It's horrible. It's tragic. My God, Sam. I'm so proud of you for what you've done with your life, coming from that. I hope you're proud, too." She ended on a choked breath. "You're amazing. Incredible…"

"Shh." His hands moved to her face, brushing at tears, then her shoulders, barely touching, his fingers fluttering. She pressed herself against him, wrapped her arms around him, held on. He went still and stiff, not yielding to her offer of comfort. She couldn't stop crying.

She wasn't just falling in love, she already had. With a man destined to break her heart in a way no one had. She'd loved Randall, but nothing like this. He'd challenged her intellectually, had appreciated her professional capability. Theirs had been a partnership of the minds, tempered with friendship and a warm, gentle love.

But Sam… Sam challenged everything—her emotions, her vision of the future, her ideas of a relationship, her view of herself. It was crazy. They'd spent so little time together, yet she knew he was the love of her life. And he was hurting so much.

His arms finally came around her, but not too tightly; he brushed his lips against her hair. He seemed calm, controlled.

At peace.

She swiped at her tears and nestled closer, not willing to let him go. She loved him. The idea settled. Wouldn't that little detail surprise him.

"I got your shirt wet," she said after a while.

"I'll add the laundry charges to the bill."

She laughed a little.

"You're tenderhearted," he said. "I don't think everyone knows that."

"It's a detriment in politics, especially for a woman. I strive for warm but professional in public."

"You succeed." His hands on her shoulders, he took a step back. "Pager," he said, unhooking it from his belt and pressing a button. "It's from Nate. A third note arrived."

"What did it say?"

"'On Monday night everyone will know what Randall did.'" He glanced her way. "Something happening then?"

"I'm presenting an award to Lilith at a banquet."

"Widely attended?" he asked.

"A few hundred."

"Public."

"Extremely. Television and newspaper coverage, I'm sure."

"So, we have two days."

"With nothing to go on." Dana waited for him to add something comforting, but his pager toned again.

"'A credible lead,'" Sam read aloud.

The words gave her hope.

Eleven

The next morning the phone woke Dana from a sound sleep. She grabbed the receiver after the second ring, eyeing the clock at the same time. Nine o'clock? She'd slept until nine o'clock? She sat up, abruptly awake, and said hello.

"Do you have something to tell me?"

Dana let her shoulders loosen. "Good morning to you, too, Lilith." She balled some pillows behind her and leaned back, yawning.

"What? Oh. Good morning. What's going—"

"How are you feeling?" Dana asked, interrupting, trying to set the tone.

"Huh? Well, to be honest, grouchy. My husband hasn't let me out of bed for three days except to move to the sofa. And now my best friend has a new boyfriend and didn't bother to tell me. I had to read about it in the *Chronicle*."

"What page?"

"What pa—? I don't know." Her voice was clipped. "Hold on."

Dana listened to the sound of pages being turned. Anticipation whirled.

"First section, page seven."

"Photograph?" Dana asked, wondering how Sam was going to feel about it.

"Yes. In fact, there's only a photo, and a caption. You're holding hands with Sam. It says, 'Senator Dana Sterling attended the funeral yesterday of Ernest Giannini, a family friend from her hometown of Miner's Camp, California. Pictured with her is Sam Remington, formerly of Miner's Camp.'"

"Is it a good picture?" She was toying with Lilith until she could get her own feelings under control.

"Oh, sure. You look swell together."

Dana's hands were tied. She couldn't tell Lilith that Sam had just been doing her a favor. If she trusted anyone, it would be Lilith, but Dana couldn't expect Lilith not to tell her husband, and Jonathan was one person too many to include.

"He does seem to be the right height for me," Dana said, still playing.

Two beats passed. "You're enjoying this way too much."

She smiled at last. "I am, actually. I'm having the time of my life."

"You said you weren't going to see him again."

"I changed my mind." She kept her voice light. "He's fun."

"Sam Remington is *fun*?"

"He makes me feel alive, Lilith. Do you know how long it's been since I've felt like that?"

"Is that all there is to it?"

"What do you mean?"

"Is he really a love interest? Or is something else going on?"

Dana wished she could share, but she couldn't. She wondered, though, if she would be forced into it soon, if anything had turned up on the TV news this morning. She'd called a Sacramento aide late last night and asked him to watch the eleven o'clock news for her. He reported later that they hadn't covered the funeral. "Like what?"

"You tell me."

How much to reveal? "I called Sam after the reunion and learned he was working in San Francisco. We've been together quite a bit since." There. No lie.

"You didn't say a word to me at my dinner party. You told me I could start setting you up."

"I'd only seen him once at that point. Anyway, you don't like him, and it's a new relationship that may not go anywhere. I wanted to keep it to myself."

"Yet you were photographed in public, holding hands. You're more careful than that, Dana, so it seems to me you're making a point. People have been waiting to see who you would end up dating. Why Sam?"

Lilith was right about everything. What point was she, Dana, making? Sam had intended only to force Harley's hand—but it had gone beyond that. Way beyond that. They'd made love. Wonderful, satisfying, please-can-we-do-it-again love. "I like him," she said to Lilith. "And that's all I'm going to say on the subject."

"Are you sure that's all there is to it?"

"For heaven's sake, Lil. Give it a rest. I had my doubts about Jonathan, as you'll recall. I gave him a chance. You could do the same, you know. Besides, this agitation can't be good for the baby." Her call-waiting alert beeped. She was grateful. "I've got another call. Can you hold on a sec?"

"I'll just say goodbye. Dana, if Sam makes you happy, I'm happy, okay? Honest."

"Okay. I'll see you at the banquet tomorrow night?"

"If my husband the warden lets me out of my cell. Bye."

Dana clicked to the other line. "Hello?"

"Good morning."

Ah. The call she wanted. "Good morning, Sam."

"Did you sleep in?"

"I did. Just woke up, as a matter of fact. How about you?" Yesterday she'd awakened and he was there in the room, a lovely memory.

"I just woke up, too. Nate called to say our picture is in the *Chronicle*."

She couldn't tell from his tone of voice how he felt about that. "Lilith just told me. I haven't seen it yet."

"My guess is it's in the *L.A. Times,* too, which presents a problem for me. I can't be in on the interview with Jordan James if he thinks you and I are seeing each other. He'll jump to his own conclusions."

Jordan James, nicknamed J.J., was Randall's former roommate at Stanford and campaign manager for all eight elections. He was currently the head of Clarity Studios in Hollywood, a failing movie-production company. Rumor had it he was about to sign on to run the campaign of Dana's same-party opponent, the one she wasn't going to throw her support to. J.J. had offered to take over Dana's reelection campaign, but she'd put him off with the same answer she gave everyone, that she hadn't made up her mind.

"What are you going to do?" Dana asked Sam.

"Arianna will be wired. Plus, she'll have an earpiece so that I can ask questions through her."

"When do you think you'll be done?"

"Depends on his answers. Anything new there?"

"I miss you." That's new.

She was greeted with silence.

"Hilda is always off from Sunday night to Wednesday morning," she said, disappointed at his lack of response but still determined to break down more barriers with him. "If you're back in time tonight, I'd like to make dinner for you." *Please say yes. Please—*

"I'll have to let you know later."

He sounded both rushed and distracted. She tried not to take it personally. "Okay," she said cheerfully.

"If you need to go anywhere today, you'll let Nate take you."

"Yes, sir."

"One more day, Dana."

One more day. It sounded like a death sentence.

Sam hung up the phone. "I miss you," she'd said, the words flowing over him like warm, scented water.

He sat on the edge of his bed, his arms resting on his thighs. She'd cried for him. He didn't know how he felt about that. He wasn't used to open sympathy or the freedom that had come when he'd finally told her about his father.

They'd barely spoken during the rest of the drive to San Francisco. He hadn't kissed her goodbye either, but had stopped at her house only long enough to pick up Arianna and head to the airport. He wasn't about to kiss the client in front of his partners.

Arianna had pronounced him "gloomy" and took advantage of the break to catch an hour's sleep, leaving him alone with his thoughts. His thoughts turned to making love with Dana. How she felt in his arms, how she looked when pleasure overtook her, how her touch both soothed and aroused. She'd given herself freely, holding nothing back, then curled into his body and slept.

He'd held her for a long time, satisfying his own needs, easing away from her only when he was in danger of falling asleep himself. They couldn't spend the night there, not with his car in the driveway.

As it turned out, they'd been lucky not to have her parents walk in on them naked in her bed.

God, he'd felt like a teenager again, being taken aside by her father to walk outdoors after dinner. They were only missing the cigars for their man-to-man talk.

"So," her father had said. "You met up again at the reunion?"

Sam forced a civil response. "That's right."

"My girl's come a long way."

"Yes, sir, she has." A preemptive strike was called for, Sam thought. Bring up the subject first. See what the man wanted without letting him circle the issue for half an hour. "Just as you predicted on prom night."

The tactic caught Mr. Cleary off guard. He clammed up for more than a minute. "We liked Randall. He was reliable. He was good for her."

Implying that I'm not? You can't hurt me that easily anymore. "She seemed to have a pleasant marriage," Sam said. *I'll bet the reliable Randall didn't make Dana moan like I did.*

Mr. Cleary eyed him as if unsure of what to say. Maybe he thought Sam admired Dana and Randall's marriage. But to Sam, "pleasant" wasn't a word that fit well with "marriage." How could you spend fifty or sixty years being "pleasant"?

"Yes, I think they did have a good marriage," Dana's father said at last.

To hell with being tactful, Sam thought. This would end right now. He stopped walking, then waited for Mr. Cleary to stop as well. "Sir, I appreciate your love for Dana, but you were wrong to warn me away from her fifteen years ago, and if that's your plan again for tonight, you'd be wise to hold your tongue. I don't know what you've got against me, but I've come a long way, too. And your daughter's capable of making her own decisions."

Damn, that felt liberating. He waited what seemed an eternity for a reply.

"Ernie said you were a pistol," Mr. Cleary said with a slight smile, extending his hand to Sam.

He shook it, his head high and shoulders back. Yeah, he had come a long way.

Sam rubbed his hands together as the memory faded. He glanced at the wall where he'd taken down Zo-onna, the Noh mask he'd given Dana. Still hanging was its partner mask, Heita, the face of a brave warrior, his sunburned skin depicting time spent on the battlefield. He looked even more fierce without the balance of Zo-onna's peace, calmness and purity.

He didn't regret giving the mask to Dana. He just hadn't realized how important Zo-onna was to Heita until she was gone.

Several hours later, Sam sat in a nondescript car on the street outside Jordan James's Hollywood Hills home and monitored the conversation inside. It had worked out well to have Arianna interview J.J., after all. The man obviously liked her—or he was doing a convincing job of getting her to think he was the last honest man in America. She'd arranged the interview by saying she was auditing Randall's campaign contributions for the last two elections. J.J. had somehow surmised she was from the state Franchise Tax Board, although she never said so and he didn't asked for identification. Fool, Sam thought, at the same time grateful. Arianna had presented copies of all the official tax documents, however, so it had been easy to mislead him. He hadn't even questioned why she was working on a Sunday.

In truth, the campaign contributions hadn't sent up any red flags, but the fact J.J. was about to take over as campaign manager for Dana's opponent led her chief of staff to conclude that J.J. was the best potential suspect. He knew Randall well enough to know his secrets; he knew Dana well enough to know she would do anything to protect Randall's reputation. Plus, he wanted his own guy in office, returning himself to the political arena while bailing from a dying business before it went under completely, destroying his reputation.

"Did Mrs. Sterling participate in a lot of fund-raising events?" Arianna asked from a list of questions designed to ease into personal issues.

"She wasn't Mrs. Sterling until after Randall was elected to his second term as senator."

"Was she an asset?"

"She might've been, if he'd lived and if he'd run for another term."

"If?"

"He was making noises about quitting. He would've had twenty-four years in Congress by then. Time for fresh blood."

In the car Sam snorted. Randall Sterling was a career politician. Quit? No way. His power would have been cemented in Washington by then, his reward chairing his choice of A-list committees, maybe even being elected leader. Dana said he'd hinted at running for president. He had the ability and the charisma to win.

"I know this is completely off topic of the audit," Arianna said conspiratorially, "but, just between us, what do you think of Senator Sterling's chances for reelection?"

The silence that followed probably meant J.J. was gauging Arianna's ability to keep the information "just between us."

"If she runs," he answered.

"Is that in doubt?"

"She hasn't announced yet."

"Are you saying she's not going to?" Arianna asked, pushing.

"I'm not saying anything."

He must have implied more with his expression than words, because Arianna said, "Ah. You're not at liberty to say."

"Perhaps we could discuss this further over dinner tonight, Ms. Alvarado?"

Arianna had a body worthy of a sculptor's re-creation and she wasn't hesitant about using it in investigations, with many successes, which only fueled her cynicism toward men and their "think with the brain in their pants" shortcomings. She'd done her homework on Jordan James and knew he had a weakness for busty women, so she'd gone to the interview dressed in a business suit but with her blouse unbuttoned to a distracting level. She'd perfected the art of crossing her legs so subtly, so elegantly, it seemed provocative. Sam had witnessed grown men transform into drooling idiots. Not that Sam didn't appreciate a woman's efforts to entice him, like Dana unbuttoning her jacket in her bedroom, revealing a bit of her black lace bra. He'd appreciated that a whole lot.

"You giving him the full treatment, Ar?" Sam asked.

"Yes, of course," she answered. "I'd love to have dinner with you, but I have to fly back to Sacramento tonight to file my report. I'm free now for lunch, however. As long as we don't discuss the audit. You understand, don't you?"

Sam chuckled. She'd nailed J.J. to the wall. She would lead the conversation, and by the end of the afternoon Jordan James would go home hornier than a soldier at the end of boot camp but drained only of information deftly culled over a simple lunch.

A lethal weapon, Arianna Alvarado. He was glad she was on his side.

Twelve

At eight o'clock that evening Sam half listened as Arianna related the day's events to Nate over a glass of Fumé Blanc and a tray of imported cheese and sourdough baguettes. The paperwork provided by Randall's accountant and lawyer was stacked on Dana's library table to be returned. Although a more complete analysis would be necessary to be a hundred percent positive, in their best judgment they could eliminate finances as a cause for blackmail.

Unless Randall had secret bank accounts, which seemed unrealistic, given his net worth.

Sam stared into his wineglass. He believed the man was squeaky clean, a rare quality. In the course of investigating someone, Sam usually found a bit of information the subject wouldn't want revealed. He could dig further into Randall's life but what would it accomplish? Private indiscretions? He doubted it, and time was too short for Sam to spin his wheels.

The focus had to be on Dana alone. Someone didn't want her reelected. But why?

The door opened, interrupting Arianna's dramatic reenactment of J.J.'s moves to lure her back to his house and into his bed. Nate was laughing. Arianna looked haughty.

"Oh," Dana said, stopping in the doorway. "I didn't know you were back." If there was an accusation in the words, Sam didn't hear it, but she moved her left shoulder in that way she had, making him pay attention to what was behind the words.

"Hilda said you were working and not to disturb you," Sam said, rising and pulling out another chair. "Join us?"

"Thank you," she said as she sat, her dark eyes studying him.

He resisted kissing her, which he ached to do. Once again she looked fragile. Lack of sleep? Worry? Him? He wanted—needed—to see her strength again.

"How did it go?" she asked as Nate passed her a glass of wine.

"We think he's all talk," Arianna answered.

"And hands," Nate added.

Arianna shoved him. Dana looked puzzled.

"J.J. got amorous," Sam explained to Dana.

"Tried to. I don't think he's your guy," Arianna said. "He's pretty straightforward. If he wanted you out of the race he would've come to you with whatever information he had. He knows how the game is played. He would have tried to convince you to drop out for the good of the party or the state or the country. Whatever. I don't get any sense at all that he's playing games with you. He misses the cachet he had as Randall's friend and campaign manager. His life stinks at the moment. That's all, I believe."

Dana spun her glass around and around by its stem but her focus was on Sam. "Now what? You must have plans or Arianna wouldn't have returned with you."

"She and Nate are going to stay in town through tomorrow, just in case. But I don't know what else we can do at this point except wait and see what happens. I'd rather be proactive than reactive, but there doesn't seem to be a new avenue. Unless there's something else you've thought of?''

Hopelessness flickered in her eyes for just a moment. ''No.''

Arianna stood, draining her glass as she did. ''I'm getting a good night's sleep,'' she said. ''Can you give me a ride to the hotel?'' she asked Nate, who was never slow on the uptake.

''Sure.'' He tucked some bread and cheese into a napkin to go.

''You're not staying here?'' Dana asked.

''We've imposed enough.'' Arianna hugged her. ''You've got the banquet tomorrow night, right? We'll be there. And before then, if you need us.''

Nate said good-night as he passed by. Then they were alone.

She said nothing.

''What were you working on?'' Sam asked.

''What? Oh, my speech for tomorrow. I'm presenting an award to Lilith.'' She sipped her wine. Her color was coming back.

Sam leaned toward her. ''What happens if there hasn't been a resolution to this mess by the banquet? Do you want to skip it?''

''Absolutely not.''

''Even if this person shows up there?''

''I'm not giving in to blackmail.''

''Even if what he or she has to say wipes out all the good you've accomplished?''

''Even if.''

He admired her guts.

She rubbed at a spot on the table. Curious, Sam waited. She seemed to be building up to something.

''Did our making love mean anything to you?'' she asked.

Only everything. He held the words inside, protecting both her and himself. He still had a job to do. A critical job. She was interfering just by being there, because she distracted him. "Of course it did."

"You haven't even kissed me hello."

He hesitated too long as he tried to figure out her mood. She pulled back just as he leaned toward her. "Not out of some sense of obligation, okay?" She pushed herself up, moved away from the table. "When did this get so serious, Sam? Thursday night we laughed together, kidded each other. I liked that. Now you hardly look at me."

"I look at you, but I've got a lot on my mind, Senator."

"Senator," she repeated. "I used to like how you called me that, in a playful kind of way."

"Playful? Are you sure you're talking about me?" he asked, hoping to lighten the mood.

Her mouth curved slightly. "Fun. Challenging. Intense."

"You make me sound much more interesting than I am."

"I left out sexy," she said, coming toward him. "I like how competent you are. I admire how you keep your promises. I love your protectiveness." She tugged on his shirt. "Feel free to chime in here with reciprocal comments anytime."

Her nerves were showing. Put her on the Senate floor and she took command. But here, with him, insecurity continued to haunt her.

Maybe because he wasn't giving her any reason to feel secure? Maybe because he couldn't? The relationship would end when the threat was resolved. It might as well be sooner rather than later, before they were in any deeper than their moment stolen out of time yesterday.

He wasn't one to sugarcoat anything. This relationship had been born out of a particular need and fueled by old dreams. It wasn't a combination that promised staying power.

"I've always admired you," he said finally, knowing it

wasn't what she wanted to hear. "I find you exhaustingly sexy, and I don't know how you could doubt that after yesterday."

"Exhaustingly?"

He smiled. "Yeah."

"Stay with me tonight."

"I can't."

She looked away, her retreat more powerful because it wasn't physical but emotional.

"I need to work," he said. "I've got to review what I know and figure out what I've missed."

"I can help with that."

"Not this time."

A tap on the door prevented her response. Dana took a step back. "Come in."

"Ma'am," Hilda said, her hand still on the doorknob. "Dinner is ready."

"Thank you. Please don't delay your trip any longer, Hilda. I'll take care of the dishes."

"I'm not driving to Stockton tonight, ma'am."

Sam felt Dana's surprise. "You aren't?"

"My daughter and son-in-law took the children to Disneyland."

"So, you're just going to hang around here?"

"Is that a problem, Senator?"

"No. It's fine. You can serve dinner, thank you."

"None for me, Hilda," Sam said quickly. "Sorry. I'll be leaving in a few minutes."

"Very good, sir."

The door closed with a quiet click.

"You can't even stay for dinner?"

He only recognized this woman from television, the woman who asked and answered tough questions on camera, whether witnesses at committee hearings or reporters.

Sam understood her better than she thought. Understood why she was drawn to him. He'd rescued her in the past, and even though they hadn't seen each other in years, he was familiar. He was also the first man to make love to her after years of loneliness. It was natural that she would form a strong attachment to him. Natural, but not real. Not for the long haul. She would find out soon how many men were interested in pursuing a relationship with her, that she would have choices.

"I'll call you in the morning," he said and watched her eyes become banked coals.

"I'll be at the office."

"Will you have to field questions about our newspaper photo?"

"I'll handle it."

While he was glad to see the fire in her eyes, he hated parting like this. "Okay." When she said nothing, he grabbed his briefcase and headed to the door.

"So, was it sympathy sex or carpe diem?" she asked before he turned the knob.

"Don't do this, Dana."

"I've been away from the dating scene a long time. I'm just trying to figure out what my expectations should be."

"It just happened, okay? No plan. No ulterior motive."

"No future?"

"I can't give you answers right now." God, he had to get out of here. Her hurt was a living thing, breathing like dragon's breath between them, so he left rather than get into a battle of words with her. He took long strides to the front door, then jogged to his car.

Didn't she know he couldn't let his feelings interfere with his job—and his job was to protect her?

And they say men are dense about the opposite sex.

Dana found the table blindly with her hand and lowered herself into a chair. She was so confused by him. They'd made love. To her that was a step forward. To him, back, apparently.

Hilda knocked then entered at Dana's call.

"Dinner, ma'am?"

"I'm not hungry after all, thanks. I'm sorry for your trouble."

The older woman started to back out, but Dana stopped her.

"In all the time I've known you, you've only missed taking your days off one time—the week that Randall died."

"I'm taking my days off. I'm just taking them here."

Dana studied her. Sam had planted the idea that Hilda could be involved in the blackmail and Dana had disregarded the possibility. Maybe she shouldn't have.

"I'd be happy to pay for a trip down the coast," Dana said. "You've worked extra hard the past couple of days."

"If I wanted to go, I'd pay for it myself. Ma'am." She left without waiting to be dismissed.

Out of character, Dana thought. Even her tone carried an edge of belligerence, unusual for Hilda. Combined with her not leaving the house, it made Dana suspicious.

No. It was crazy. What could Hilda gain by Dana not being reelected?

She rested her head in her hands. She was so tired she couldn't think straight. She'd thought the demands of her job were exhausting, but they were nothing compared to this emotional roller coaster. Maybe she shouldn't give up her career. Maybe she should just stick to the job and forget having a personal relationship. They were too painful. Too confusing. People die or walk away. Either way it hurt too much.

Which was ridiculous, of course. She wanted to get married again. She wanted children. One of the reasons she wasn't running for reelection was so that she could have a family and not be flying coast to coast all the time.

Forcing herself to climb the stairs to her bedroom, she took a long, hot bath, then slipped into her robe. She closed the closet door on the new negligee hanging on the inside hook, a sheer red number with lace appliqués in the critical spots.

She opened the double doors to her balcony and stepped outside into the cool evening. The breeze from the bay lifted her hair, chilling her bath-warm skin. Below her was the courtyard where she'd shared her first kiss with Sam. She shivered. Rubbing her arms, she turned around to go back into the bedroom. Directly in her line of sight was the mask Sam had given her. She'd taken down her wedding picture and put Zo-onna in its place.

Drawn to it, she lifted it down from the wall and sat on the bed, laying the mask in her lap, running her fingers over it. A century old. How had he found it? Did he buy it specifically for her or did he already own it? If so, why would he give her such a treasure? It was too much payment for her keeping his medal all those years, which cost her nothing.

His generosity continued to surprise her, especially since he'd grown up in a house where generosity was nonexistent after his mother's death. His most precious gift, however, was sharing his past with her. She didn't know if she was the only person other than the Gianninis that he'd confided in, but she knew it had taken a lot for him to—

Dana sat up straight. He'd confided in her, told her the worst about his past.

He trusted her, and, in a way, that seemed more intimate than sex.

What did it mean?

What did he fear most? Rejection? His father had a hand in that. Abandonment? His mother, through no fault of her own, played a part there.

Dana had kept her love for Sam to herself, hoping he would come to love her as well. But maybe he was just waiting for her to say it first.

Maybe he *needed* for her to say it first.

What time was it? After midnight. She shivered again, but this time from anticipation. From her closet she grabbed jeans, a T-shirt, baggy pullover and a knit cap. She examined her image in the mirror when she was dressed. Would anyone recognize her? Her hair was down around her face and held in place by the cap pulled low on her forehead. No makeup. She couldn't find her sunglasses anywhere so she added ultracontemporary, dark-framed reading glasses that no one had seen her wear in public. So what if her vision blurred? She only needed to get from the car to an elevator to his room.

She grabbed her wallet and keys and hurried out of the room, down the stairs and out to the garage. Instead of the Lincoln, she drove her Mustang convertible, a treasured leftover from her Cal days, her high-school graduation gift from her parents. In no time she arrived at his hotel. She gave up trying to find parking and turned the car over to a valet attendant, who let her know she had to be a hotel guest to park there. She gave Sam's room number, hoping the valet didn't recognize her. He was too young to care about politicians, she supposed, and she did look different.

She kept her head down through the sumptuous lobby, then bounced nervously as she rode the elevator to his floor. Her reflection in the mirrored walls startled her. She looked happy and hopeful, which were both true. She wasn't going to try to seduce him, but to tell him she loved him. No pressure, just the facts. She hoped it would make him as happy as it did her.

His door was at the end of the hall. It was so quiet as she walked that she could hear her own heart beating like something out of Poe. Just when she reached his door, it opened, making her step back.

He stood there, dressed in jeans and a sweater, a set of keys in his hand.

"Did you just come from Haight-Ashbury?" he asked, his eyebrows lifting.

She did look reminiscent of the hippie era, she realized, although cleaner.

"Sam." Her voice shook. It was all she could do not to blurt out her feelings. She took another breath and tried again. "May I come in?"

He stepped back and opened the door, tucking his keys in his pocket, then shutting the door behind her.

She looked around the sitting room, not really seeing much. "Sam." She stopped, started again. What if he rejected her? "You can refuse what I'm offering or you can accept it. I don't have any control over your choice. But you're not leaving this city and my life without knowing how I feel. I—"

He put his fingers to her lips. Before she had a chance to come up with the right words, he backed her against the door and kissed her, long and deep and hard, with a kind of desperation that stole her breath. He dragged her cap off her hair, plucked her glasses off and tossed them onto a nearby chair.

"I couldn't work," he said between kisses. "I kept thinking of you. Wanting you. I was just leaving to come to you. I'm sorry about tonight," he said as he peeled her pullover up her body then flung it aside.

"Me, too," she whispered back, shoving his sweater up and over his head, tossing it in the general direction of hers. What she had to say could wait. She wanted this. Needed this.

He framed her face with his hands. His eyes held her captive. "I didn't want this to happen. I need to focus because I'm missing something big, and I can't shake the feeling I'm missing it because I can't free my mind of you, of worrying about you. But I need you. This."

"I'm glad," she said, warmth infusing her. "I'm so glad."

"God." He hauled her close, held her for a long time, then he backed away and undressed as she watched.

"Let me be the one this time," she said, giving him a shove toward the bed.

She liked how he stretched out, waiting, watching her, not closing his eyes when she knelt over him. She liked how he tasted and how he felt, hard and soft at the same time but differently. He was hot against her tongue. He moved in short, sharp lifts. His hands clenched the sheet. She liked that, too, and the sounds he made...

She offered him pleasure with a heart full of love but without obligation. What will be, will be. But he wouldn't leave without knowing what it meant to be loved by her.

His fingertips pressed into her head, stopping her before she was ready to stop. "I have to be inside you," he said, dragging her over him, fisting her hair in his hands, finding her mouth in a wet, open kiss that lasted forever, changing directions, deepening by the moment, the longest kiss she'd ever known.

When she couldn't catch her breath, she sat up, straddling his hips, and pulled her T-shirt over her head. She was naked underneath.

"How unsenatorial," he said, covering her breasts, circling his thumbs around her nipples. He drew her down until he could taste her. "You feel so damn good, Dana," he said, rough and low. "But your jeans are killing me."

"I'm sorry." She tried to move off him.

"No. They don't hurt. The rubbing against me... and you moving. It's more than I can..."

He let the words trail off as he sat her up and unzipped her pants. "Why, Senator Sterling. No panties, either."

"I was in a hurry."

"Uh-huh." He flipped her onto her back and moved down the bed. "Hiking boots? When was the last time you went hiking?"

He dragged his tongue along the skin revealed by her open zipper as he plucked at her shoelaces.

"In college," she said when the first boot hit the ground. "Once."

He laughed, low. "Well, the outdoorsy look suits you, in case you were wondering."

"I was worried."

The other boot bounced on the floor, then his gaze turned serious again as he pulled off her jeans along with her socks. He settled between her legs and put his mouth against her, sliding his hands under her, lifting her, dipping his thumbs inside as he worked his magic with his tongue. She couldn't remember ever feeling so free. She had no doubts, no hesitation. Again and again he brought her up, pulling away just before she was about to crest only to take her up again and higher. He had her begging. Still he controlled the moment until he was ready to let her soar.

And soar she did, almost beyond consciousness.

She didn't come down all the way but leveled off still needing him. She pushed him onto his back again, climbed over him and lowered herself to his hips. She leaned down, letting her hair drift over his chest.

"Protection?" she asked, nipping at an earlobe.

"In the dresser. Top drawer."

She walked across the room, aware of him watching her, feeling desired and desirable. When she started back with the packet in her hand, he raised up on his elbows.

"Stop," he said.

For a moment she was afraid he was going to back out, then she recognized the heat in his eyes. He just wanted to look at her. As foreplay it worked amazingly well.

"Come over here," he said, his voice gruff.

"Need something?" She smiled, moved forward, straddled him again, unrolled the condom down him. He held her by her hips, lifted her onto him, lowered her slowly, both of them holding their breaths until he was deep into her, stretching her beyond what she thought possible. He helped her find the rhythm, then his eyes glazed.

"I love you," she said as she exploded from inside, shattering her world while finding a new place for her at the same time. With him.

He stopped momentarily then gathered her close and rolled with her, staying connected until he found his own release, his breathing labored, his muscles hard.

He didn't relax against her but climbed out of bed and went into the bathroom, shutting the door. Dana sighed, at peace. He could be angry or wary or frustrated by her announcement but she wasn't going to let him chase her away. She pulled the sheet to her shoulders.

She heard the water run then stop. Some time passed. When he came out, he had a towel wrapped around his waist and a robe over his arm. He sat on the bed, facing her, and passed her the robe. He'd splashed water on his face.

"This is what I've been afraid of," he said.

Ignoring the robe, she smiled, feeling serene. "I'm not apologizing. I love you."

"You're attached to me because of the circumstances."

"That's why I can't sleep? Can't eat? All I think about is you." She wasn't going to let him get away with rationalizing her feelings. They were hers and she had a right to them.

"It's the circumstances."

"It's love."

"I'm the first man you've been with for years, that's all."

"Bull. I haven't been with anyone because no one interested me. Until you. I'm not expecting anything from you. This is a purely selfish gesture. I need you to know how I feel, because if this is the last night I have with you, I'm not going to spend my life regretting that I wasn't honest."

"I think you should get dressed and go home."

She settled back into the pillows. "I'm not going anywhere. I'm sleeping with you tonight. I'm going to make love with you at least two more times. I'm going to make you whimper."

She finally succeeded in wiping the doomsday expression from his face. "Whimper?"

"Oh, yeah."

He looked interested. She sat up, letting the sheet fall to her waist. "I know you're confused," she said, climbing to her knees and wrapping her arms around his neck. "A part of you wants to throw me out and never see me again, because I shake up your world too much. Another part wants to have sex right this second, because making love with someone who loves you makes the sex so much better.'' She kissed him, tenderly, lovingly. ''And yet another part of you wants to spend the night in my arms, talking and confiding and comforting and being comforted, because that kind of intimacy has been missing from your life. By your own choice, no doubt, not because other women haven't loved you.''

''No one has.''

''I'll bet you're wrong. You scared them away, that's all.'' She pressed a kiss to one eye then the other, his temples, his jaw, and finally his lips, which clung to hers harder than she would have expected. It gave her hope. ''Well, you can't scare me.''

''I need to keep sorting through my notes,'' he said as she reached between them and pulled the towel away. ''I'm missing—'' he hesitated as she climbed into his lap, facing him ''—an element in the equation.''

''Later,'' she murmured. ''Much, much later.''

He settled her against him. ''You're expecting a lot out of me this soon after—''

''I am.'' She laughed, low and warm. ''Tonight you're all mine.''

And tonight was a good start.

Thirteen

She had made him whimper.

Sam recalled the moment with bemusement. Dana slept, her cheek against his chest, his chin resting on her hair, her leg tucked between his, as if they'd slept together a thousand times. Her perfume was masked by the soap from their shower, but she still smelled like Dana.

He'd lost track of the number of times she said she loved him. At one particularly vulnerable moment he'd voiced his fear. "You're only making it worse."

"For you or for me?" she'd replied.

He suspected for both of them, but before he could answer she framed his face with her hands and looked deep into his eyes. "Don't try to tell me how I feel. If this is all I get, I'll take it and be happy with it. But is it enough for you?"

He'd been inside her at the time, so rational thinking wasn't in play. At that moment what they had seemed enough. But now? In the dark of night with her breathing softly and her trust so obvious in the way she slept soundly in his arms? He didn't know.

And was he thinking relationship...or more?

He needed to be done with the job so that he could see the big picture again. Before she'd arrived at his hotel room, he'd charted everything he knew about the case, evidence and speculation. The answer was there. Somewhere. Earlier he hadn't been able to focus on it for worrying about Dana, how he'd left her at her house. He could think now, knowing she was here, safe.

Sam eased out of bed, pulling the covers over her shoulders, tucking the pillows around her. She made a sleepy sound, but didn't awaken. He scooped up his robe from the floor and shrugged into it, then gathered his papers. He hadn't bothered to turn off the light in the sitting room before they fell asleep. Settling there, he tried not to rustle pages.

He ran down the list of most obvious people who wouldn't want her to run for office, most of the names provided by Abe, the reasons why they would be suspect listed, as well as the reason for their elimination. In some cases, only a name was written down because they didn't have enough information to say yea or nay. That list included her same-party candidate as well as the one from the opposing party. Sam put red stars next to their names.

Dana must have enemies. A spurned lover of Randall's. A former employee. A colleague. Randall's lawyer had provided names of women who'd had long-term relationships with Randall but could offer no reason why they wouldn't want Dana to continue Randall's legacy. Two of the women were married and had children now. One he couldn't track down.

A separate page listed people with personal rather than political motives. The list was short. First, Hilda. He added a red star to her name because Dana told him how this was only the second time Hilda hadn't taken her days off. Did she need to be home on Monday to complete something she'd started? What possible reason could she have?

Then there was Harley—a star by his name, too, but not a red one. He presented a different threat...

Sam went still. He underlined Harley's name, then again, his pen slicing the paper. A different threat, but tied to the original?

It made sense. It made perfect sense.

His pulse revved.

"You should be too worn out to be thinking." Dana's voice was husky with sleep and sexy as hell. She stood in the bedroom doorway, naked and beautiful.

Deciding not to share his speculations with her, he tossed aside the papers and approached her. She smiled leisurely.

"Something you want, Senator?"

"Well, as long as you're up," she said, her smile taking on a sultry curve. She walked her fingers down his chest, untied his robe then kept going. "Or will be soon."

"You're insatiable."

She looped her arms around his neck, drawing him close. "Lucky you."

Dana bit back a groan as she stepped into her office at 7:00 a.m. Her in-basket held a foot-high stack of paperwork. She'd noticed an equivalent pile on Maria's desk, as well, which would make its way onto Dana's before the day was done. Not to mention anything else left over from her staff because of her absence on Friday.

She tucked her purse into her bottom desk drawer, hung up her jacket and dug into the stack. Maria had arrived before Dana and soon brought coffee and a few minutes of conversation about her weekend. Abe came in shortly thereafter, and they met with the door closed for a few minutes.

After Abe left, Dana leaned back in her chair and let herself think about the night in Sam's hotel room. She'd chipped away at some of his resistance, she thought, but far from all of it. He was back to his intense self this morning, a man with a purpose, although he didn't tell her what that purpose was, only that he would be investigating a new angle. He kissed her goodbye with an unexpected fierceness, then walked her to the hotel garage at 5:00 a.m., reminding her that he'd meet her at her office parking structure to follow her home after work. The banquet started at 6:00 p.m. with a no-host bar, then dinner at six forty-five, followed by the awards and presentations. He would drive her there.

What happens after tonight, Sam?

The question dogged her. If the day went by without any action on the threat, would he leave, figuring it was just a hoax? If they discovered who was behind the plan, would he turn everything over to Abe…and leave? She didn't win either way.

He hadn't even asked what her plans were for when her term expired.

Her chin in her hand, Dana tapped her pen on the desktop. She'd lied when she said she'd be happy with last night, but what else could she do? She couldn't hold him against his will. After they'd dealt with the blackmail they would have time to concentrate on them.

Maria came in.

"I'm done with those," Dana said, pointing to three folders.

"Okay." She tucked them under her arm. "There's a man in the lobby who says he's a friend of yours. A Harley Bonner. His name doesn't show up on the master list."

No, it wouldn't. He hadn't contributed. And he wasn't a friend.

"Ask Abe to step in, would you, please?" Dana said to Maria. *We'll let Mr. Bonner cool his heels a little while.*

"Do you want to call Sam?" Abe asked after they'd talked.

"I want to keep Harley waiting but not that long. I don't even know what Sam's up to. He's got something going."

"I can stay."

"I don't think he'll open up if you do. But I want to close my door so that no one else hears what's going on. Let's leave the intercom open between my office and yours. That way, you can monitor. Maybe you should tape our conversation?"

"Illegal without telling him."

She stared at him.

"But, okay," he added.

Dana waited until Abe said he was ready then she sent for Harley. He carried his hat and wore a white western shirt, complete with pearl snaps and a bolo tie with a silver steer-horns clasp. It was hard to believe he was only a year older than she. He'd aged infinitely more, carrying weight that was no longer muscle, his ruddy face lined. He'd been a good-looking and surprisingly popular boy in high school, yet Sam, who'd had a monstrous upbringing, had turned out much better than this pillar-of-the-community's son.

"Hello, Dana," he said amiably, twisting his hat in his hands.

Politeness? What's this new game, Harley? She didn't stand nor did she offer her hand. "Have a seat, Harley."

He looked around. "Nice."

"Out of my seven offices, I like this one best." She took pleasure in reminding him of her status. "What do you want?"

"Look, I know we got off on the wrong foot at the reunion."

Dana leaned back. She held a pen in her hands and turned it over and over. "Did you honestly believe there would be a 'right foot' between us?"

"Bygones. You know. A lotta time's gone by."

"Some memories never die."

"Be that as it may, the reason I asked you to dance at the reunion was to talk to you about the bill you've been workin' on in the Senate."

"Which one? I'm working on a number of them."

"The one from the agriculture committee."

"You mean the Subcommittee on Marketing, Inspection and Production Promotion, of which I'm a member?"

"I guess."

"Done your homework, have you, Harley?"

"Look, you know which one I'm talkin' about so don't go lookin' down your nose at me."

"Are you referring to the trade act? The one which, among many other points, opens up more foreign markets for livestock sales?"

"That's it."

"What about it?"

"It's comin' up for a recommendation when you go back to Washington. I want to know you're sayin' yes."

"You think I'm likely to share that information with you after the way you accosted me after Mr. Giannini's funeral? Called me names? You've certainly changed your tune."

"I apologize for that, but your personal feelings shouldn't get in the way. That bill is important to the cattle industry, which is big in this state. You represent the interests of this state."

"I'm not the only vote."

"From what I hear it's split. Your vote makes a difference. I'm askin' you, Dana. I'm askin' you real nice. A lot of people's livelihoods are dependin' on you makin' the right decision."

"And if I don't?" She goaded him on purpose. *Let's see how far you'll go.*

"It's gonna hurt my business bad. And bad for me is bad for Miner's Camp, and all those people I employ and the taxes I pay."

"Well, now, Harley, I'll bet if I got into your IRS file I'd see you haven't paid a whole lot of taxes. You probably got subsidies because of drought or flood or fire. Some dramatic disaster, anyway. I'll find huge losses instead of profits. And didn't I hear Candi say your ranch is the eighth largest in California? Wasn't it number three or four while your father was alive?'' *Come on. Threaten me. Give me a reason to have you hauled off.*

His face flushed redder. ''We've had some hard times since my father passed.''

''Nothing you say will influence me. Nothing.''

He stood. She put down the pen and folded her hands in her lap.

''Look, little lady, if you think to vote no on this to spite me—''

''You give yourself too much credit. My vote will be determined solely by what I believe is best.'' She stood as well. ''You've overstayed your welcome.'' Dana figured dismissing him would push him over the top.

He planted his hands on her desk. ''Don't forget I know somethin' about you that a lot of folks would find interestin'.''

''That's a tired threat.''

''You watch. You'll be sorry.''

Abe rushed in the moment Harley was gone. ''Do you want him stopped?''

''For what? He didn't make the threat specific. Nothing would stick. Did you get it on tape?''

''I headed in here as soon as he started to threaten you. I'll have to go check.''

''Okay. I'll give Sam a call so that he can come listen to it. Thanks, Abe. It was good knowing you were there.''

''You handled him like a pro, Senator. I'm sorry you won't be staying on.''

It had felt good to be in the driver's seat, she realized. Whoever had sent her the threats had stolen that freedom from her this past week. She didn't ever want to lose that control again.

In his car, Sam listened to the tape over the telephone, his fury at Harley tempered by his respect for how Dana handled him. The Senate was about to lose an amazing woman, someone who brought poise and equanimity to the job. He wondered whether her mind could be changed—

"Sam? Did you hear all that?" Dana asked.

"Yeah. How does he know the vote is split?"

"Industry lobbyists. They conduct informal polls. Do you still believe he's not behind the letters?"

"I don't know. Maybe he is. Maybe he was just seeing how you're doing with the Monday deadline. Figured you'd be so scared you wouldn't come to work. At least we know he's in town and can look for him tonight, shut him down before he makes any public statements."

"He'll be as out of place at the banquet as my attending a wrestling federation match, don't you think?"

"Harley's not self-aware enough to consider it," he said in the understatement of the year. Sam pictured the look that must've been on Dana's face when Harley called her "little lady." "I bet he slunk out of your office with his tail between his legs."

"I don't think it's long enough."

Sam laughed.

"Well, there were rumors in high school," she added. "So, what are you up to?"

"Waiting for a chance to interview someone."

"Who?"

"I'll tell you later. I might be completely off base. Call me if you need me."

"Okay."

"Dana? Thanks for last night."

Her momentary silence gave him time to remember the details.

"My pleasure," she said.

He heard the smile in her voice before he ended the call. She hadn't said she loved him this morning. When the sex ended, those three little words stopped, too. Wasn't that a guy thing?

Sam glanced in his rearview mirror as a car approached then turned into the driveway of the French Normandy-style house where he was parked. The home had the same view as Dana's. In fact, it was only a couple blocks from Dana's, although it wasn't as magnificent nor as large. Still, the building had a grace that suited Lilith Perry Paul perfectly—conservative, traditional and elegant.

He climbed out of his car and walked up her driveway. She still sat in her car, had probably spotted him in her rearview mirror.

He came up to the driver's-side door. She keyed the power to roll down her window.

"I heard you were on bed rest," he said, seeing not fear in her eyes but perhaps wariness. He remembered Dana saying that he scared Lilith. He wondered why.

"My husband's idea, not doctor's orders. In fact, I just got back from the doctor. She said I'm fine. What do you want, Sam?"

"Answers."

"To what questions?"

"Has Harley been threatening you?"

Shouldn't have looked away, Lilith. Sam didn't need to hear her answer to know it was yes. Plus, she'd gotten so sick she'd taken to bed during what Dana said was a normal pregnancy. One plus one equals—

"Harley Bonner?" she asked, smoothing out her face. "Heavens no. Why? What could he threaten me about?"

"Only you would know the answer to that." Maybe a little matter of some drugs? "Let me phrase it another way. Is he blackmailing you?"

She laughed. "Good grief, what a question, Sam. My life's an open book."

"Dana thought hers was, too."

She looked visibly shaken. "What? Harley's black-mailing Dana?"

"Appears so."

"How much money does he want?"

Ah. "Over what?" should have been the first logical

question, but it wasn't. "He wants her not to run for reelection."

Lilith looked away again. Her fingers curved over the steering wheel more tightly. "Why?"

"That's the question. We're not sure."

"Are you sure it's Harley?"

"He's the likeliest candidate." *What's going on, Lilith? What do you know?*

"I knew something was up. I knew it. I even asked Dana if—" She clamped her mouth shut.

Her hurt that Dana hadn't confided in her was palpable. "Lilith."

She looked at him, her expression wiped clean of emotion.

"Dana told me you don't like me much. I accept that." He leaned closer to the car. "But you *can* trust me. I'm only interested in getting to the truth and protecting Dana. I'll do what it takes."

"I can't tell you anything, Sam. I'm sorry."

Can't or won't? She wasn't guilt free, but guilty of what?

"You need to leave now," she said.

He straightened. "I'll see you tonight at the banquet."

Her surprise lasted only a second, then she nodded.

He retraced his steps to his car, noting that she didn't leave hers until he was pulling away. He added one more name to his list: Lilith. How could he tell Dana that?

Fourteen

Dana loved formal banquets. Loved the sound of silverware clinking against china, the smell of floral perfumes mingling with musk, the sight of beautiful garments and glittering jewelry and tuxedos, the feel of a handshake, whether limp or bone crushing, clueing her in to someone's personality. Laughter always punctuated a low buzz of nonstop conversation until a gavel sounded or a bell rang. She loved it all. But then, she also liked potluck dinners and county fairs. You can take the girl out of the country…

Randall had called her his secret weapon at his fundraising events because she so obviously enjoyed attending. As a team they could work an entire room, even during a short event. She'd always been proud of what she'd brought to him, not only as his wife but his partner.

The fact this evening's banquet was a Business and Professional Women's League event meant there were many more women than men, so the pitch level of the conversation buzz was higher and the fare lighter. Tonight's offering featured puff pastry–wrapped salmon with capers and herbs, rice pilaf and steamed vegetables. Over dinner Dana chatted with the president of the BPWL to her right and the recipient of the Small Businesswoman of the Year Award to her left. On the far side of the president sat Claire Cavanagh, an Emmy Award–winning actress who played the CEO of a Wall Street brokerage firm on a popular night-time soap opera. Dana had no illusions about who was the bigger draw to this event. Most women admired Claire's portrayal of a high-powered woman succeeding in a man's world.

Dana cherished the company of women, particularly bright, smart, forward-thinking women like these. She almost relaxed for a while.

Sam had been quiet on the drive to the hotel venue. She'd asked him if he'd discovered anything, but his reply was a noncommittal "Still working on it."

Since he hadn't kept her out of the speculation loop before, she was baffled by his silence. While she mingled during the cocktail hour, he huddled with Nate and Arianna, examining the three notes once more, then Sam said something emphatic, stabbing at the notes, and Arianna nodded and Nate looked unconvinced. All three surveyed the room constantly. Soon they separated. Dana knew they were connected by a high-tech communications system.

She thought it was overkill. The threats hadn't indicated a potential for physical harm. Although not obvious, the place was crawling with security provided by the hotel, standard for events like these, and it seemed like enough, but Sam didn't want to involve them unless it became necessary, which was fine with Dana. Usually an aide accompanied her, referred to as her "body guy," but even he had been left out of the picture this time.

Her presentation of Lilith's award would be last. Dana had condensed her speech to a one-page outline, and before dinner she tucked the folder containing the outline in the shelf under the podium so she wouldn't have to carry it from her seat, always an awkward moment. It had been fun reminiscing about growing up with Lilith.

The speeches began. A local comedienne warmed up the crowd then gave the Image Award to the actress Claire Cavanagh for her skill in presenting a successful business-woman in a favorable light—if you disregarded her char-acter's four marriages and most recent affair with her step-son. The show was a soap opera, after all, the comedienne reminded everyone, and Claire's role as a television CEO was still one to emulate.

After Dana was introduced, she made her way to the podium, smiling at Lilith as she retrieved her folder and opened it. The top sheet wasn't her outline but a note on the same heavyweight cream-colored stationery as the three previous letters.

Last chance, the note read.

He was here. In this room. Now. He'd seen her put her folder in the podium. Watched her. Was stalking her.

Dana sought Sam in the darkened wings. "I'm a little embarrassed to say this," she said into the mike, her eyes on him, "but I gave my reading glasses to a friend for safekeeping and forgot to get them back." It was their agreed-upon I-need-you-right-now alert.

Sam came across the stage, his strides long and quick. Forcing a smile, she discreetly passed him the note. He read it then indicated with a nod that she should continue with her speech, at the same time taking out her glasses from his inside pocket and handing them to her. He walked away a little more slowly. Dana made a point of watching him.

"Actually, I didn't forget them," she added with a wink to the audience, even though she felt far from flirtatious. "I just wanted to watch him walk away." Sam played the game by looking over his shoulder at her and grinning, shifting the audience's response from laughter to applause with hoots and hollers. If anyone wondered whether the news photo had captured a romantic relationship between them or just old friends from the same hometown comforting each other at a funeral, they wouldn't be wondering now.

Dana put on her glasses, unnecessary with the large font she'd used to type the notes. "Good evening. I'm so pleased to have been invited to present this award tonight, especially since I didn't have to research the recipient before writing her introduction. You see, I met Lilith Perry the summer before seventh grade, just after she moved with her family to my hometown of Miner's Camp. Because the start of the new school year was three months away, she needed to figure out a plan to meet new friends right then. She decided to take a page out of the comic strips and set up a booth in her front yard that she hoped would draw people to her. Her sign read, *Advice: twenty-five cents.*"

Laughter rippled through the room.

Dana took off her glasses and held them, making her next words seem unplanned. "Your fee's gone up a little since then."

Again, there was laughter as Lilith toasted her.

"As I recall," Dana continued, "your logo was a rendering of the classic theater masks, except you used those yellow-and-black smiley faces, one smiling, one frowning."

She faced the audience again and waited for them to quiet. *Where are you, coward?*

"The result was glaring but admittedly eye-catching. I saw the sign from my mom's car as we drove to the grocery store. On the way back, I made Mom drop me off at Lilith's house.

"I was her first client."

What are you waiting for? A better time to embarrass me? You have everyone's attention right now.

"You see, I was desperate to know how to get John Carruthers away from Jenny Packard. I couldn't ask my mom because she was, like, *old.* I couldn't ask my only cousin because he was a guy, and therefore, like, *ignorant.*"

The teenage lament brought smiles. Dana had to consciously form hers.

"So I took my this-is-surely-the-end-of-the-world problem to Lilith, laid it on the card table for her, desperation in my voice, my need for him like potato chips and soda to my survival. I wanted John Carruthers. I wanted him *bad*."

She paused for laughter, her stomach churning. The anticipation was killing her.

"Lilith listened. Pondered. Then spoke like the Dalai Lama on the tip top of a mountain, intoning his wisdom—'Grow breasts,' she said."

As the audience roared she saw Nate stick his head through a door and gesture to Arianna, who hurried to join him in the outer reception area. Sam didn't budge from his post. He stood like a Secret Service agent, constantly scanning. She knew he'd planted himself at the best vantage for a lone person to view the crowd, if necessary.

Dana needed a sip of water but decided her hand would shake too much. She went on. "Anyone who's listened to Lilith's radio program knows she's still giving that same unflinching advice.

"What many people don't know is how much she gives to the community." She slipped on her glasses again, using the prop she'd made a point of needing, then listed Lilith's many accomplishments, ending with, "She hosts her own talk show five days a week and many times has been known to stay on the line with a desperate caller after the show ends."

"And now she must have discovered she has too much free time on her hands, so she decided to have a baby to pick up the slack."

Dana came to the end of her speech. What would that end bring?

She lifted the cut-crystal award shaped like a fire's flame.

"It is my honor and privilege to present this year's Cass Schroeder Award for exceptional service to the community to my best friend and all-around good person, Dr. Lilith Perry Paul.''

The audience came to its feet. Dana almost dropped the award as she passed it. Lilith struggled with it as well. As the people on the stage gasped, Claire Cavanagh raced forward to steady Lilith, then took the award and set it on the table beside the podium, making a joke that sounded as if it came from an echo chamber, as did the laughter.

Dana caught Lilith watching her with an expression more serious than Dana had ever seen in all their years as friends.

Lilith touched her hand. ''Dana—''

''Shh.'' She wanted to scream, the pressure was unbearable. The blackmailer had so little time left to make his accusations in a public forum—Lilith's acceptance speech, closing remarks from the BPWL president, then it would be over.

Screaming not being an option, Dana hugged her friend a little harder then returned to her seat. She didn't hear Lilith's talk, only the words she emphasized about giving back, serving, self-satisfaction. About education, fulfilling work, a supportive husband and good friends.

Dana watched Sam. Her heart thundered in her ears. She was aware of Lilith taking her seat again and the president returning to the podium, but heard nothing except an incessant pounding. Then Sam was behind her, his hands on her shoulders. He bent low. It must have seemed like a loving gesture to anyone watching.

Was it over? Had it been a cruel joke someone had played? A hoax?

''Nothing happened,'' she whispered, confused.

''I need to talk to you,'' he said quietly.

Dazed, she stood. He put his arm around her waist, for which she was grateful. Then as they were about to walk by Lilith, he cupped her elbow and said, ''Come with us, please.''

''What's going on?'' Lilith asked. She scanned the area. ''Where's Jonathan?''

"He'll be along shortly."

Were they both in danger? Dana wondered. Was it Harley, after all? It was the only common denominator Dana could think of between her and Lilith.

Sam took them into what appeared to be an empty storage room and closed the door.

"Lilith needs a chair, Sam," Dana said.

He tipped his head back and swore, making her jump. "Even now she thinks of you first," he all but shouted to Lilith.

"What—" Dana looked from Sam to Lilith. "What's going on?"

"Are you going to own up? Or shall I tell her?" When Lilith said nothing, Sam pulled out the four blackmail notes and handed them to her. "They're typed in the same font you used for the invitations to the party you threw for Dana's election—on the same damn paper—that Dana has framed in her sitting room."

Disbelief and horror spread through Dana like bad whiskey, burning, nauseating. "No," she said. "No."

Lilith stared at the notes for a lot longer than it took to read them. She put her shoulders back and turned to Dana, looking belligerent and devastated at the same time. "I'm so sorry—"

"No! It's impossible." She grabbed Sam. "You're wrong. You're so wrong. Lilith would never do this to me. If she had a problem she would come to me… You would come to me, right?" Dana whispered, facing her friend.

Tears brightened Lilith's eyes. "Harley threatened to expose my drug use, not just the marijuana but the other things, too. He wanted two things to keep quiet—money and for me to convince you not to run for office again. He's got all his hopes tied up in another candidate, one who promises to help him. He knew if you ran you would win. He's about bankrupt, you know." The words poured out of her without a breath, so that she was panting at the end.

"That's a lie," Sam said. "I had him checked out."

"Well, he told me he was. How was I to know any differently? The money meant little in comparison to what having my past exposed would mean for my career."

Dana's world had righted itself at last and she could think. "I do know what it would mean. I also know your heart. You would never do this to me," she said, positive of her words. She stepped closer to Lilith. "Jonathan, maybe. But not you."

They stared at each other. Lilith trembled. Dana gripped her arms to steady them both.

"Did you know what he was doing?" *Please say no. Please—*

"In his own way he was trying to protect me," she whispered, not making eye contact, her voice shaking as much as her body.

She *knew*? Hurt sped through Dana in liquid fire, incinerating what remained of her innocence, her belief in basic human goodness. She watched the person she'd shared so much of her life with become a stranger. A pregnant stranger, she reminded herself.

"She needs a chair," Dana repeated over her shoulder to Sam, who with obvious reluctance left the room. "Tell me, Lilith."

Tears spilled down her cheeks. "Harley came to me after the reunion threatening to tell the tabloids what happened that night in your car and what else he knew."

"How did he know about it?"

"I bought the stuff from a friend of his. He made it his business to know. He probably didn't imagine I would go to Jonathan with his threat, but there's nothing I don't share with my husband. I'm where I am now because of him, professionally and personally." She pulled a tissue from her pocket and blew her nose.

"I told Jonathan I would tell my listeners myself before I'd let Harley leak it to the world. And I certainly didn't want to involve you."

But you did involve me. Dana was so confused. "Were you really sick?"

"Yes! Worried sick. That was no game. Dana, I kept asking you if something was going on. You were acting so strangely, but you kept denying there was anything happening, so I finally decided it was just me projecting onto you or this fling with Sam, or whatever that relationship is. Then Sam came to my house today and asked if Harley was blackmailing me. I couldn't figure out how he knew until he said that you were being blackmailed. He thought it was Harley, but I knew it had to be Jonathan. I'm not apologizing for him, Dana, but I understand the way his mind works. He would do anything to protect me. Anything. Haven't you ever been desperate?"

"Yes. Ever since I got the first letter." She ignored Lilith's flinch. "I thought someone had some horrible secret that would tarnish Randall's name forever. But whatever that secret was, I wouldn't have covered it up if it meant hurting someone innocent."

"I didn't know," Lilith insisted. "I didn't put it together until Sam planted the idea in my head. I immediately accused Jonathan. He didn't deny it. He said he figured it was worth a shot. He didn't have anything on Randall, you know. Did anyone? But he thought it might provoke you into announcing your decision, one way or the other, so that we would know where we stood. That's all he wanted, for you to make your decision public."

"So, because he didn't have any intention of following through on the threat he sent to me, that makes it okay?"

"No. Of course not. I'm not trying to justify what he did, only telling you why he did it."

Where was Sam with that chair?

"Did you ever consider coming to me, Lilith? Telling me what was going on? Did you think I wouldn't have helped?"

She looked at Dana as if she'd lost her mind. "After what you did before—taking the blame for me? Being taken to the police station? Standing before the chief? Lying to your parents? Going to the rehab classes? I was already in your debt. How could I ask anything of you?''

''Because we were friends.'' As far as Dana was concerned, that said it all.

''Were?'' Lilith repeated, panic in her eyes.

''I understand you didn't know what Jonathan was doing until today. But there *was* today, Lilith. You could have told me today.''

''I thought it was over, that Jonathan had given up.'' Fresh tears glistened. ''I decided that confessing to you would cause more harm than good, that once the deadline came and went you would chalk it up to someone's awful idea of a joke and forget about it. Yes, it was the coward's way out, but you've never cared for Jonathan....'' Her voice trailed off, as if she saw the absurdity of what she was saying.

When she spoke again, her voice was calm. ''I had no idea he was going to plant that note tonight. He must have hoped it would be your final straw, that you would announce your decision out of fear tonight.'' Lilith squeezed Dana's arms. ''If he'd asked me I would've told him you were too strong to give in to threats.''

Dana pulled back. ''Just as Sam didn't talk to me about his suspicions about you. I would've convinced him he was wrong, too.''

Lilith ventured a smile. ''How is it that two such independent women are attracted to such protective men? We don't need taking care of, do we?''

Dana found no returning smile to give her. ''You're the psychologist. You tell me.''

''I'm afraid of the answer.'' She took a step away. Her hands settled protectively over her belly. ''I'm going to tell my radio audience about my past. I hope they understand why I've never said anything before. But if they don't, I'll live with it. My life will still be full.''

''Telling may damage your credibility,'' Dana said. ''But

it also may make you more human. You'll be talking from experience.''

''Leave it to you to see the bright side.''

Yeah. Leave it to me. Little Mary Sunshine.

The door opened. Jonathan was escorted in by Nate and Arianna. Sam followed with two chairs.

Jonathan didn't even glance in Dana's direction. He went straight to Lilith. ''Sweetheart, are you okay?''

''I'm fine.'' She leaned away from him.

''You're not fine.''

''I am.''

Dana clamped her mouth shut, but her mind screamed, ''What about me? Does anyone care about me?'' She read the plea in Lilith's eyes. ''Go home,'' she said, wanting her gone, knowing there was nothing left to say.

Sam roared to life. ''Like hell.''

She turned to him, her voice calm. ''The decision is mine.''

His eyes went cold. ''Yes, ma'am.''

Dana understood his anger. He'd fought a battle and won. Now the guilty were being set free without a trial, even though all the evidence was there and fairly gathered.

''I think we're not needed here any longer,'' Arianna said to Nate as soon as Lilith and Jonathan left. ''Senator, I hope to see you in the near future.''

''Likewise,'' Nate added.

''Thank you,'' she said. It was all she could manage.

After the door shut, Dana and Sam faced each other.

She hadn't seen this side of Sam before, the controlled but escalating fury. It turned his eyes to steel and his jaw to granite. Had he grown a few inches? He looked huge. Imposing. Powerful.

''Dana.''

She expected anger. Accusation. Frustration. But he said her name with such tenderness. She couldn't make it fit with how he looked. Confused, she shut her eyes. She felt him move closer. He said her name again. She opened her eyes and he was there, right in front of her, her knight in shining armor yet again, offering her sympathy. Understanding. Caring. The world moved in slow motion as it caved in around her, dragging her into a deep, dark pit. "Oh, God, Sam. She was my best friend. My best friend. How could she do that?"

He wrapped her in his arms, stopping her from falling into the pit. She fought tears, not wanting to seem weak. He liked her strength. Admired it and her—

"Cry," he said into her hair. "Just cry."

After a minute she realized she wasn't crying only because of Lilith but because of Sam, too. There was no reason for him to stay—and every reason for him to go, before her public presence complicated his life beyond repair.

"Let's go," he said at last.

She should have felt better now that the threat was resolved, but a different kind of fear settled in and refused to budge.

Fifteen

Sam felt Dana's gaze on him as he drove her home. They'd barely spoken since leaving the hotel. He didn't know what to say. The job was over. Time to deal with the real issues.

"One of the things I admire about you," she said into the quiet, "is your tenacity. I knew you would find the needle in the haystack. I knew you would find who was behind the letters, even with so little to go on."

"I wasn't so sure." He glanced at her. "You were magnificent during the banquet."

"I was petrified."

"Courage isn't about not being afraid. It's about how you handle your fear." He slowed for a stop sign. "Why aren't you running for reelection?"

"You know, I was thirty years old when I took office," she said, weariness in her voice. "The minimum age for a senator. I hadn't held public office before. My only qualification was that I'd been married to a man who'd served almost twenty years in Congress."

"You have advanced degrees in political science. You worked in his office for years, wrote his speeches, were part of his policy-making strategies. And you've done a good job on your own."

"But it's *all* I've done. I've lived it. Breathed it. I run seven offices and employ seventy people. I have to study harder, know more, and at the same time not rile anyone, plus defer to those who've been there longer, who've proven themselves, even when I think they're wrong."

"You would prove yourself, in time." He had no doubt about that.

"But most senators build up to their position. I didn't. There was resentment about that, but because Randall was so popular and I was a young, grieving widow, no one hassled me. Not publicly. This time around, the gloves would be off."

"You can handle that."

"I don't want to handle that."

"Ah."

"I thought I knew what the business of politics was about. The compromises you have to make. The games you have to play. Some people learn how to work the system and still accomplish their goals *and* keep some of their ideals intact. I'm not ready to compromise, I guess. I'm not ready to let go of some of the principles I cherish."

"What will you do?"

"What I always wanted to do. What I studied so hard for. I'm going to teach. At the university level." She leaned toward him. "And I haven't told another soul about this, but I plan to run for the Senate again in another twenty or twenty-five years."

The idea pleased him. "You'd make the record books."

"I wouldn't mind that. I'd like to leave a legacy for future generations."

She'd left the words hanging out there for him to react to or ignore. He chose to ignore them. A minute later they were pulling in to her driveway. He didn't turn off the engine.

"You're not coming inside?" she asked quietly.

"I can't." He willed her to understand.

"I know," she said, then her expression turned more intense. "Why not?"

Because she would push him for answers he couldn't give her—answers she wouldn't want to hear. He didn't believe what she felt for him was real, but he knew she couldn't see that yet. Soon, though. And he didn't want to be around to hear her try to say she'd made a mistake.

"Why did you let Lilith and her husband go?" he asked instead.

She frowned at the change of subject. "What good would come from pursuing some kind of punishment? Are you mad at me because I didn't punish them? Is that what this is about? Because if anyone has a right to be angry, it's me. I had a right to know about Lilith. You should've told me you suspected her."

"When? Before the banquet, when I wasn't sure? I didn't make the connection of the typefaces until we were there. It would've ruined your evening whether I'd been right or wrong. I wanted to be wrong. I'd hoped Harley would burst into the room so that I could have the pleasure of hauling him off."

"I wanted the same thing."

She put a hand on his arm. He didn't want it there, a reminder of what he was giving up, because he knew her. *He knew her.* Knew that just as in high school, she had a new life ahead of her, one he couldn't be responsible for slowing down. It wouldn't take long for her to realize her feelings for him were nostalgic and ephemeral, tied up in the moment of confusion and mystery that they'd just experienced.

"There's something I've wanted to know for a long time," she said.

"What?"

"Why were you able to rescue me from Harley before? Why were you there?"

He ran his hand along the dashboard, brushing away nonexistent dust. "Right place, right time. I was on my way to your house. To say goodbye." Needing to avoid her father, he'd been waiting down the road when he'd seen Harley's truck pull off into a well-forested area. He thought he saw Dana in the passenger seat but wasn't sure, so he followed.

"Goodbye? *Before* graduation?"

"Classes were done. I'd officially graduated. I wasn't hanging around an extra day to sit through the ceremony."

"Then I went to the police," she said. "And Harley and his buddies came after you."

He shrugged. He didn't want to rehash it anymore.

"Why did you come to the ceremony, then? Everyone could see you'd been beaten."

"To show Harley he hadn't won. Then—"

She waited. "Then what?"

"You wouldn't even look at me." That was the worst. She hadn't once looked his way. Hurt and angry, he'd left her the medal so that she wouldn't forget him. Because of that medal they'd come full circle. He had to say goodbye again. Leave her again.

"I told you, Sam. I was protecting you. I figured I had time to make it up to you. I didn't. You left town without telling anyone you were leaving. Then when you showed up at the reunion, I thought I had a second chance to set things right, but I hadn't expected to fall in love with you."

Don't tell me that. "You reacted to the situation," Sam said, keeping his voice level when he wanted to shout. Nobody falls in love that fast. Nobody. He knew what drove her to think she had. But in time she would forget him, just like before. He had to find a way to end it right now, even if the truth hurt.

"You became dependent," he said, sure of his words.

"Then you transferred that dependency into something else. Infatuation, or whatever you want to call it."

"I'm not a teenager. If I say I love you, I do. Did last night mean nothing to you?"

"Last night was great. I already told you thank-you." Just get out of the car and walk away, he told her silently.

"You shared your secrets with me. Your pain," she said quietly, her voice strained. "You gave without asking anything in return. You made me stop looking back and inspired me to look to the future." Dana leaned close to him. "I know it seems fast, but it doesn't make it any less real."

"You'll see."

"At least come in for a nightcap," she said. "It's hard talking in the car."

"I can't. I'm going home."

"Home? To L.A.?"

He nodded.

"Now? Tonight? But you have your car. You would have to drive." Dana heard her voice go shrill and tried to tone it down. "It's already past eleven. By the time you check out of the hotel—"

"I already checked out. My luggage is in the trunk."

The proverbial ton of bricks fell on her. He'd known he was leaving. He'd planned it.

"I never figured you for a coward, Sam."

"I guess it's a good thing you found out now." His voice was firm and factual.

Dana wasn't buying any of it. No one shares the kind of week they did only to make an about-face from concerned, gentle protector to casual, sarcastic acquaintance.

"What's going on?" she asked.

"You said last night that you'd be happy with that."

"I thought you'd give us a chance once the threat was gone and we were living normal lives again. You're not going to give us a chance?"

"I'm telling you, Dana, that you've created some sort of fantasy. We had some unfinished business, that's all."

''That's not all, and you know it.''

''You're grateful.''

Her jaw dropped. ''Whoa. This is a side of you I haven't seen. When did you become Mr. Chauvinist? I thought you respected me.''

''Exactly my point. You don't know me. How can you love me? What you're feeling is temporary.''

''What if it isn't?''

He didn't hesitate. ''I don't feel the same way you do.''

He couldn't be any more clear than that, but oh how it hurt. Tears burned her eyes. She refused to cry in front of him.

She opened her door. ''Have a good life.''

If he said something she didn't hear it. The front door seemed a mile away. She focused on it like a life raft after a shipwreck. She didn't hear his engine start, so he must be watching her until she was safely inside, ever the protector.

Had she confused love with a strange kind of dependency? With lust? With infatuation?

She picked up her pace, needing to be away from his all-seeing gaze. The life raft still bobbed too far out of reach.

Had she wanted the fairy-tale ending so badly that she saw only his heroic qualities? She'd had a comfortable relationship with Randall. She wouldn't have a comfortable relationship with Sam.

But she'd thought she could have life instead. Passion. A partner in the best sense of the word. Someone willing to argue...and make up. Have babies with.

Love her.

She reached the door, shoved the heavy wooden portal open and almost fell inside. She pushed the door shut and leaned against it, covering her face with her hands.

Love her.

Sam would challenge her. Believe in her. She could tell him her fears. She wouldn't have to be right all the time. In fact, he would take great delight in telling her when she was wrong. And he could bask in her own love, unwavering and infinite.

Why didn't he want that?

"Ma'am?"

Dana pushed away from the door, swiped at her tears. "Hilda. What are you doing up?"

The older woman came a little closer, her white robe glowing in the dim light of the foyer. "That Mr. Caldwell came here tonight after you left for the banquet and wanted something from your sitting room to take to Mr. Remington. I tried to call you at the hotel but I couldn't get through to you. Was it okay?"

Dana sighed. "Yes, it was fine."

"I didn't like doing it without your permission."

"It's all right, Hilda. Is that all?" She wanted to be alone. She was never alone.

"Mr. Remington isn't with you?"

"No. Why?" Her patience was as brittle as spun sugar.

"I just wondered how many for breakfast."

"Just me. Just me forever," she snapped, then regretted her tone instantly. "Look, I'm really tired. I'm going to bed." She walked past Hilda, reached the bottom step of the staircase.

"I was hoping he might be around awhile, ma'am."

It took Dana a few seconds to absorb Hilda's words, so rare was it that she offered a personal opinion. Dana stopped on the fourth step and turned around. "Why?"

Hilda hesitated. "I just— This doesn't seem to be a good time for a talk."

"Lay it on me." How much worse could her night get?

"I was hoping, ma'am, that he'd be the one."

"Why?"

"Because he made you happy. And because I'm ready to retire. I didn't want to leave until you were settled."

Dana plopped onto the stairs. She stared at Hilda in amazement. "I didn't think you even liked me."

Hilda's eyes softened. A small smile touched her lips, surprising Dana.

"The reason I'm still here is because I like you. I've been waiting for you to find someone and get married again. I didn't want to leave you alone. But I want to spend the rest of my years near my family. My grandchildren. I'll stay until you find someone, of course, ma'am."

"Of course," Dana repeated, watching Hilda disappear down the hallway. She pressed her face against her legs to muffle the hysterical laughter that threatened.

After a minute she continued up the stairs, making a mental to-do list: 1. Hire new housekeeper (probably going to need three people to replace Hilda). 2. Get over Sam.

She stopped in her bedroom door and studied the room, then revised her list: 1. Sell house and find much smaller place. 2. Get over Sam.

Sixteen

Sam wanted a shower, a steak and twelve hours' sleep. He punched his alarm code into the panel outside his front door, then lugged his gear inside. The silence assaulted him. After a month of nonstop business on the East Coast, he was home at last, but not until he'd endured a five-hour weather delay at Logan Airport.

He kicked the door shut behind him, dropped his garment bag and briefcase on the landing, then went directly into the kitchen, where he grabbed a beer from the refrigerator and a steak from the freezer, tossing it onto the counter. He took a long swig of beer as he headed to his office. No new messages—just the ones he'd saved from Dana.

She'd called twice during the month. She could have called on his cell phone, but she'd chosen to call at home, probably assuming he wouldn't be there to pick up. The first time she apologized for the media attention. People were speculating about them having broken up before they were really an item, as well as wondering who he was.

He pushed the Playback button to hear the second message for the fiftieth time, a message he still hadn't deleted: "I love you, Sam. If you believe nothing else in this world, believe that."

That message had gotten to him more than anything else. Not only the words, but the emotion in her voice. She hadn't left a message in the two weeks since.

His finger hovered over the Erase button. After a minute he headed to his bedroom, stripped down, then moved toward the bathroom.

Catching a glimpse of the Noh mask, he stopped to raise his bottle to it and the empty space beside it before taking another long swallow. A minute later he stood under a hard spray of hot water. He dragged some shampoo through his hair and soap down his body, then he leaned his hands against the tile wall and let the water beat his shoulders and back. God, he was tired. Tired of work. Tired of being alone.

Tired of missing Dana. Tired of telling himself he didn't.

His dreams were full of her. His arms were empty of her. He expected the ache to have faded by now, but it had only gotten worse. He'd caught her on C-SPAN purely by accident at three o'clock in the morning a couple of days ago in a taped committee hearing. Her August recess over, she was back in Washington. He could picture what she wore under her suit.

He couldn't stomach the idea of her with another man. He couldn't imagine life without her by his side. He would tell Nate and Arianna tomorrow that he was going after Dana, if she didn't toss him out on his ear. He'd leave the firm if he had to.

The doorbell rang as he stepped out of the shower. His bell never rang unless he was expecting someone, and the last thing he needed was a Girl Scout selling cookies. Cursing, he hastily dried off then pulled on a pair of shorts and a T-shirt. He yanked open the door and went numb, except for a violent lurch of his heart.

"Dana."

She looked beautiful. Her hair was down and in a new style that took the senator look off her. She wore big hoop earrings, a bright pink V-neck pullover that showed some cleavage, and formfitting pants that emphasized her long, lean legs.

"May I come in?" she asked, hesitation in her eyes and her voice.

Holding the door handle, he backed away, giving her room to come into the house. She glanced at his luggage on the landing.

"Getting back or leaving?" she asked.

"Home. After a month away." He watched her study his living room.

"This is nice," she said, turning back to him. Her smile was forced. "It suits you."

He finally shut the door and tried to pluck a coherent sentence out of the words tumbling in his head. Damn, she looked good. Rested. It struck him that maybe he had been right to let her go. She had healed—that was visible. Was living again. Did that mean she was over him? That it *had* been infatuation and dependency?

"Are you hungry?" he asked, not in a hurry for the answers to the important questions, for fear of what the answers would be. "I was just about to put a steak on the grill."

"Thank you, but no. I won't take up much of your time."

Stay forever.

"I have something to say, and it needed to be in person. Could we—" she looked toward the leather sofa "—sit down?"

He gestured for her to lead the way. She perched on the edge of the sofa, setting a shopping bag at her feet.

"You heard that Lilith went public with her past to her fans?" she asked.

"It doesn't seem to have hurt her."

"She didn't file charges against Harley."

"I heard that, too." The small talk had to be a stall tactic, Sam decided, because surely she knew he'd kept track of Lilith and Harley.

She blew out a breath. "This is harder than I thought."

It struck him then why she was there. Why she was nervous. Why she looked different. "You're pregnant," he said, his gaze sliding down to her abdomen. He wanted to cover that precious spot with his hand, to kiss her there, to—

She choked. "No. Heavens no. We used protection every time. Why would you think that?"

He shook his head, not giving voice to the fantasy he'd never allowed himself to consider outside his dreams. "I figured it had to be something important to bring you here in person."

"It is." She rubbed her hands on her thighs, then reached into the bag and pulled out a bubble-wrapped package. Carefully she set it on his lap. He knew its size and weight. It was Zo-onna. She was giving the mask back to him.

His throat closed. He couldn't look at her. She didn't want his gift.

He put it back in the bag, then shoved it at her.

She didn't take it. "I can't keep her, Sam. You know I can't."

"It was a gift."

"An expensive gift. One with particular meaning to you." She touched the back of his hand.

"Arianna told me it's one of a pair you chose specifically. She said you spent almost everything you had on a serviceman's salary to buy them."

He pulled his hand away. "How did she know I gave it to you?"

"Nate saw the mask on my bedroom wall when he got Lilith's wedding picture out of my sitting room. He told her."

"They should stay out of my business."

"They care about you."

He moved to stand by the barren fireplace. She was too calm. He'd waited too long to realize the depth of his feelings—and to tell her. "I'm not taking back the mask."

"You have to. I can't keep it." She came to stand with him.

"*You* have to," he countered, studying her, memorizing her. "It's important to me. I didn't have a clean slate with you, so I tried to make one. Your father—" He stopped. He couldn't tell her about that, not even to make excuses for himself.

"My father ruined the prom. Yes, he told me finally. I'm so embarrassed by what he did to you that night, Sam. He had no right." Her eyes darkened. "Do you know why he did it?"

"I figured he saw the way I looked at you." How could he have missed it? He'd been head over heels.

She shook her head. "He told me it was how *I* looked at *you*."

Sam went still. He could hardly believe it. How had he not seen it? "Is that the truth?"

"And nothing but."

Her father must have seen the way Sam looked at Dana, too. "Well, he loves you. He wanted only the best for you. I wasn't the best."

"He was wrong. Look at all the sacrifices you made for me." She spoke over his attempt to respond. "You took me to the prom, only to have my father blindside you. You saved me from Harley's attack, only to be beaten up because I was so stupid.''

"You—"

"Let me finish. You attended Mr. G.'s funeral with me, had your photograph in national newspapers, essentially giving up your anonymity, the thing most precious to you—your career. And now you won't even bill me for the job you and your company did.''

"I slept with you! I'm supposed to bill you after that?'' He shoved his hands through his hair. "God, Dana. What kind of man do you think I am?''

"Exactly my point,'' she said quietly. "I didn't—don't—deserve you. I finally came to understand that. And that's why I can't keep Zo-onna.''

He stared at her, dumbfounded. "Are you—'' He stopped, tried to sort through her logic. "Are you trying to say you're not good enough for me?''

"I'm good enough. We'd be good together, but I understand why you can't forgive me. You made all those sacrifices and I've given you nothing.''

"Nothing,'' he repeated in disbelief. Heat flooded him in the form of memories. "I've loved you since I was ten years old and you were the only one to offer me sympathy. Seeing you every day at school was my reason for going when it was the last place I wanted to be. Competing against you in class gave me purpose, kept me studying, made me a better student, then a better person. Taking you to the prom was the best night of my life, even after your dad talked to me.''

He cupped her face and looked into her bright eyes. "Rescuing you from Harley made me feel worthwhile after my father had done his best to make me feel worthless. Helping you find who was threatening you gave me a chance to show you what I'd become.''

"You love me?''

She'd ignored everything but his first words. He kissed her with as much tenderness as he could muster.

"I love you," he said. "I'm sorry I hurt you. I couldn't believe you loved me that fast. I didn't trust it."

"Do you now? Because I've been miserable without you, and I can't keep on waiting and hoping."

"I trust it. I believe in what we have." It didn't matter how it affected his job. He wasn't giving up Dana for anything or anyone. "You wouldn't have waited long. I was coming to see you. You always seem to beat me to the punch."

"I was more desperate than you."

"It was impossible for you to be more desperate than me." He gathered her close. "So, did you really come here without knowing whether I was in town?"

"Not exactly. Arianna told me you'd be back today."

"And did you just successfully use reverse psychology on me by pointing out your weaknesses, knowing I would defend you?"

He felt her smile against his shoulder.

"Once a knight always a knight."

"Are you going to marry me?"

She squeezed him so tight he almost lost his balance. "Well, we can't live together without marriage. That would set a very bad example."

"Then it's settled."

She angled her head back enough to meet his gaze. "No, it isn't. That wasn't a proposal. That was a business discussion."

Grabbing her hand, he walked her toward his bedroom, scooping up her shopping bag as they went. In the bedroom he unwrapped Zo-onna and hung her next to the other mask. "Heita welcomes her home."

"The warrior." She eyed Sam askance. "I've been studying."

"He hasn't been the same without Zo-onna." He paused.

"I haven't been the same without you. I love you, Dana, with all my heart. I want to have children with you. I want to make a home, wherever you want."

"Here would suit me just fine. I'd like to apply to teach at UCLA."

He was speechless for as long as it took to draw a deep breath and swallow hard. "Will you marry me and be my love forever?"

"I will. Will you argue with me and make up with me and be my love forever?" she asked in return.

"What kind of dumb question is that?"

She frowned. "It's a perfectly good question. It's important to me. Critical—"

"I'm sorry. Please forgive me." He angled his head toward his bed. "Can we make up now?"

She laughed and threw her arms around his neck, pulling him close. "Let's go to Las Vegas tonight."

"I don't think so. You need the fairy-tale wedding."

Tears coated her eyes. She settled her arms around him more comfortably, and brought her face close to his, her lips close enough to kiss. "How do you know that?"

"Anyone with a bedroom like yours at your parents' house needs the church and the flowers and the beautiful dress. It's your last wedding. It needs to be perfect."

"You won't mind the spectacle?"

"I'll see only you."

A tear spilled down her cheek. He brushed it away.

"Let's go to bed," she whispered. "I've got an engagement gift for you."

"Let's wait until the wedding night." Her shock made him smile. "I figure you can put together a big, fancy wedding pretty fast if you're motivated."

She tipped back her head and laughed. He hadn't ever heard her sound so joyful.

"Oh, am I going to drive you crazy in the next month," she said.

"A month?"

"Probably." She nuzzled his neck.

His whole body reacted.

"Well, hell," he said, then he did what he'd wanted to do since he'd first seen her at the reunion—swept her into his arms, kissed her and took her to bed. "We can start the countdown tomorrow."

* * * * *

The BEHIND CLOSED DOORS *series*
continues with Arianna's story,
HOT CONTACT,
available in June 2004.
from Silhouette Desire.

If you enjoyed what you just read,
then we've got an offer you can't resist!

Take 2 bestselling love stories FREE!

Plus get a FREE surprise gift!

Clip this page and mail it to Silhouette Reader Service™

IN U.S.A.
3010 Walden Ave.
P.O. Box 1867
Buffalo, N.Y. 14240-1867

IN CANADA
P.O. Box 609
Fort Erie, Ontario
L2A 5X3

YES! Please send me 2 free Silhouette Desire® novels and my free surprise gift. After receiving them, if I don't wish to receive anymore, I can return the shipping statement marked cancel. If I don't cancel, I will receive 6 brand-new novels every month, before they're available in stores! In the U.S.A., bill me at the bargain price of $3.57 plus 25¢ shipping and handling per book and applicable sales tax, if any*. In Canada, bill me at the bargain price of $4.24 plus 25¢ shipping and handling per book and applicable taxes**. That's the complete price and a savings of at least 10% off the cover prices—what a great deal! I understand that accepting the 2 free books and gift places me under no obligation ever to buy any books. I can always return a shipment and cancel at any time. Even if I never buy another book from Silhouette, the 2 free books and gift are mine to keep forever.

225 SDN DNUP
326 SDN DNUQ

Name	(PLEASE PRINT)	
Address	Apt.#	
City	State/Prov.	Zip/Postal Code

* Terms and prices subject to change without notice. Sales tax applicable in N.Y.
** Canadian residents will be charged applicable provincial taxes and GST.
   All orders subject to approval. Offer limited to one per household and not valid to current Silhouette Desire® subscribers.
   ® are registered trademarks of Harlequin Books S.A., used under license.

DES02   ©1998 Harlequin Enterprises Limited

SPECIAL EDITION™

From *USA TODAY* bestselling author

SHERRYL WOODS

PRICELESS

(Silhouette Special Edition #1603)

Famed playboy Mick Carlton loved living
the fast life—with even faster women—
until he met Dr. Beth Browning.
Beth's reserved, quiet ways soon had him
wanting to believe in a slow and easy,
forever kind of love. Could Mack convince
Beth that his bachelor days were over?

**The second installment
in the popular miniseries**

MILLION DOLLAR DESTINIES

Three brothers discover all the riches money can't buy.

Available April 2004 at your favorite retail outlet.

COMING NEXT MONTH

#1573 SCANDAL BETWEEN THE SHEETS—Brenda Jackson
Dynasties: The Danforths
There was one thing more seductive to hotshot reporter Jasmine Carmody than a career-making story: tall, dark businessman Wesley Brooks. But Wesley had his own agenda, and would do whatever it took to ensure Jasmine didn't uncover the scandal surrounding his close friends, the Danforths…even if it meant getting *closer* still to Jasmine!

#1574 KEEPING BABY SECRET—Beverly Barton
The Protectors
The sexual chemistry had been explosive between Lurleen "Leenie" Patton and Frank Latimer. And their brief but passionate affair had resulted in a baby…a son Frank knew nothing about. When tragedy struck and their child was kidnapped, Leenie needed Frank to help find their son. But first she had to tell Frank he was a father….

#1575 A KEPT WOMAN—Sheri WhiteFeather
Mixing business and pleasure was against the rules for U.S. Marshal Zack Ryder. But Natalie Pascal—the very witness he was supposed to be protecting—tempted him beyond reason. The vulnerable vixen hid from a painful past, and Zack told himself he was only offering her comfort with his kisses, his touch….

#1576 FIT FOR A SHEIKH—Kristi Gold
Texas Cattleman's Club: The Stolen Baby
Sheikh Darin Shakir was on a mission to find and bring to justice a dangerous fugitive who used Las Vegas as his playground. But unforeseen circumstances had left Darin with bartending beauty Fiona Powers as his Sin City tour guide. Together, they were hot on the trail of the bad guy…and getting even hotter for each other!

#1577 SLOW DANCING WITH A TEXAN—Linda Conrad
Making time for men was never a concern for workaholic Lainie Gardner. That is, until a scary brush with a stalker forced her into hiding. Now, deep in the wilderness with her temporary bodyguard, Texas Ranger Sloan Abbot, the sexual tension sizzled. Could Lainie give in to her deepest desires for the headstrong cowboy?

#1578 A PASSIONATE PROPOSAL—Emilie Rose
Teacher Tracy Sullivan had had a crash on surgical resident Cort Lander *forever*. But when the sexy single dad hired *her* on as his baby's nanny, things got a little more heated. Tracy decided that getting over her crush meant giving in to passion…but would a no-strings-attached affair pave the way for a love beyond her wildest dreams?

SDCNM0304